© Tony O'Neill

Digging The Vein

First Edition

ISBN 1-903110-18-1

Cover Design by
Owen Benwell

Published in 2006 by
Wrecking Ball Press
24 CAVENDISH SQUARE • HULL • ENGLAND • HU3 1SS

Digging The Vein

Tony O'Neill

Wrecking Ball Press

Inner notes

Digging The Vein is dedicated to my wife Vanessa for her unerring love and support in the face of my insanity. Thank you for encouraging me to write this book instead of living it. And to our daughter Nico Estrella O'Neill who is a daily reminder of how good life can get. Also to the memory of Randal P. Earnest, the craziest motherfucker I ever met, who died as he lived: at full throttle.

Thank you

Shane Rhodes and everyone at Wrecking Ball Press:
Thank you for all your hard work in putting this book out.

Dan Fante, for inspiring me through his own writing and for his invaluable advice on my own work.

These people tried to save my ass again and again: the Musicians

Assistance Program, Cri-Help, The Telesis Foundation, Todd and everyone at Clean Needles Now in Hollywood, The Methadone Alliance (thank you, Bill Nelles) and Dr. Barbak at The Marybourne Practice. All of the dealers who played the game straight and never shorted me on a deal.

And finally to all the junkies, thieves, whores, malcontents, fuck-ups, burnouts, psychos, and drug dealers: we are the last truly free men and women on this stinking cop and politician-ridden planet. It's time for everyone to Just Say No to the War on Drugs.

HOLLYWOOD, AUGUST 2000

In Hollywood, the sun rises and stays up in the dirty sky pummelling you into submission for twelve hours or so before sinking behind the hills. Then everybody waits for it to start up all over again, up and down and up and down, futile and ceaseless. No seasons, no change, just relentless brightness. Nobody can ever escape the glare of the unforgiving sun. They just carry on, dumb with sunshine and desert heat, trying to find a darkened corner where they can conduct business that has no place is the daylight. I took the metro to Hollywood and Western. The station was all done up in a gaudy, touristy faux-Hollywood style. Columns of film canisters reached up to the fluorescent white light beaming down from the ceilings. Murals of palm trees and a day-glow Hollywood sign adorned the walls. I ascended in the glass elevator to the surface and I found myself back on familiar ground. It felt good to be back into a regimen.

I followed Hollywood Boulevard West and watched my feet as they trampled the stars. Here, tourists started to slow up and turn around sensing the sudden decline in the neighbourhood. As soon as they hit Vine, the street traffic became mostly homeless kids and crack dealers. Menacing cops prowled the side streets. Wine heads loitered looking for change. Here, tourists became very aware of the cameras around their necks and the travellers' checks in their wallets as they hastily retreated to the security of West Hollywood. On the stroke of six o'clock, a troupe of Scientologists in matching light blue shirts and navy ties marched up the street from their residences and into the bedlam of the boulevard, barely making eye contact with the human wreckage swarming them. I watched them from a pay phone while paging Carlos. On a billboard above the porno theatre, a tired, sad-looking woman in a red bikini looked down at me.

At the corner of Hollywood and Vine, an old, crazy crack head with a white beard turning copper at the edges sucked on a glass stem and looked at me with wide dead eyes as I loitered in front of Ripley's Believe It Or Not. He blew plumes of white smoke like some ancient dragon, and the chemical smell hit me from twenty feet away, making my guts churn in delicious expectation. Oh, hell. Before I even knew what I was doing, I found myself walking down Vine and cutting left into the side streets to score some rocks.

Within five minutes, I was scoring in a back alley from a tall black guy who sat on the curb trying to get a hit from his pipe. He sold me two rocks and offered me a hit. I accepted out of habit, but then started to get edgy as I watched him pull the rock from a pocket of his dirty sports jacket and fumble with it, clumsily balancing it on the gauze, shaking the lighter and trying to make it work. Click … click … the lighter was dead and the crack head was pissed. He had grey hair. I wondered how old he was—forties? Fifties even?

"Mother … fucker!" he hissed, "You got a light, man?"

"No."

I started to walk off and he looked almost dejected at being left alone. He was really high, jerking spasmodically even while sitting down.

"Hey … hey!" he yelled, "Don't go, man. Wait."

I stopped and half turned, raising my palms to the sky.

"I gotta split, man. I gotta go."

"Wait … wait." He flashed me a yellow, rotting grin. "You want me to suck you a little? I'll do it for one of those rocks, my man."

Later in Greco's Pizza, I sat waiting for Carlos at a Formica-topped table. I was drinking Hi-C Pink Lemonade. A young Dominican guy slid into the seat next to mine. He wore a huge Virgin de Guadalupe pendant encrusted with fake gems around his neck and Ostrich skin cowboy boots. His grin revealed a gold tooth.

"You waiting for someone?" he asked in broken English.

8

"Yeah," I told him. "Are you a friend of Carlos?"

He smiled and pulled out a beeper. "Carlos is gone. I have his pager now. I got the stuff."

"What happened to Carlos?" I asked, slipping the forty dollars into his hand.

He shrugged and spat a balloon into his hand, rolled it on his pants leg and dropped it into my palm.

"I have his pager now," he simply repeated.

There's something in the ritual that you learn to love–opening the balloon of heroin and placing the dope into the spoon, which is stained dark brown with old heroin residue and coated black with carbon on the underside. There is a smell to Mexican black tar heroin ... caramel or treacle mixed with the smell of lost childhood summers. The smell of a strange nostalgia, of a yearning that you can't explain.

Adding water to the spoon and holding a flame under it and watching the water start to hiss and bubble, the nugget of smack dissolving, turning the water the colour of chocolate. And then there's the sound as you unwrap a fresh needle from its package, the way the cotton you drop in the spoon swells and engorges with the solution, the smell again, stronger as it rises with the heat from the cooked junk. Then the faint fizz as you draw up the shot into the barrel, turning the cotton a dirty grey once more. You become addicted to this. I have become addicted to this.

For a moment an insane thought crosses my mind–maybe it isn't too late. Maybe I don't have to inject this drug. After all, I am no longer physically dependent on it after thirty-eight days in rehab. Maybe simply preparing the shot can be enough; my overwhelming need for the ritual sated so I can go on with my life.

I put something appropriate on the CD player ... Chet Baker. Maybe *Almost Blue*. That's always good. And then I'm slipping the belt from my jeans and the cold leather is wrapping around my upper arm. Flexing for a vein, needle grasped between my teeth. I almost don't need the shot. I am already altered, transported, fixed.

I slide the needle in anyway, and shoot my way to glory. Outside of my motel room, in a dull suburb of Los Angeles less than a mile from the detox facility I checked out of last night, I can hear the cars and the yelling and feel the heat outside on the walkway. None of it can touch me now that the heroin is deep and heavy in my bones. I fall back into a trance.

I am beyond life and death, beyond the boredom and madness now. I make a mental note to myself while drifting into my opiate dream. If this ever ends, if I survive this, I will write it all down. I need to remember everything, and I don't want these years to have been for nothing.

Well, this is how it started.

PART ONE: BEFORE

I was in a band, before. We were called The Catsuits and we enjoyed a brief burst of fame during the late 90s. The music press fell for our fragile, intelligent lead singer, Laura, and the caustic blasts of Ramones-meets-the-Shangri-La's pop-punk we produced. Looking back now, it still seems as if we had it all in the palm of our hand and I still cannot see how it slipped away from us. It was tragic how unaware we were right up until the end. "The best band in Britain by a million miles," *NME* called us. A big record deal, a top-twenty single, appearances on *Top of the Pops*, a debut album that peaked at number nine in the charts. Every date on our UK tour was greeted with packed, adoring houses.

I joined the band after accosting them drunkenly at one of their shows at the University Of London Union. I was in London playing keyboards for Mark Brel, a shining light of the early 80s synth-pop revolution and the voice behind one of that era's greatest hits, an electro take on an obscure northern soul song, now some fifteen years into a solo career. During my stint as his sideman, he became more and more reclusive and withdrew almost entirely from live performing. This left me sitting in my rented room in a crumbling Edwardian house in Chelsea, collecting my weekly pay to spend on alcohol and drugs. The Catsuits show I attended was typical of my performances in London at the time: I drank straight vodka for most of the night and after the show ended, barged into the backstage area talking to all the faces I recognized from the music press as if we were on first name terms. "Your band is fucking brilliant," I told Laura, waving my arms derisively at the other music scene faces lurking by the open bar. "Much better than the rest of these assholes. You lot have *class*. Watch this ..."

I drunkenly staggered over to a guy called Simon who was the lead singer of a synth-pop outfit being hailed by *Melody Maker* as one of the most important new bands of our time. He was drinking a martini by the bar, and eyeing me with obvious distaste.

"You're Simon, aren't you?" I slurred, loud enough that the whole room could hear, *"From I Dream Of Wires?"*

"Yes" he sighed, his precious hair, and neat suit marking him out as a member of the new musical genre the press were calling The Romantic Modernists.

"Your band," I told him, "is worse than shit. It's despicable. It speaks to no one but old, out of touch *Melody Maker* journalists."

Then for my coup de grace, I took the martini glass from his hand and drained the contents with a theatrical flourish. I slammed it on the bar and yelled "Garçon! Another Martini for my friend!" before staggering back to my conversation with Laura.

"I hate that band," I said by way of explanation. "Now, The Catsuits. You know what your problem is?"

"Go on," she laughed, "I'm sure you're gonna tell me anyway."

"You need a keyboard player. But not some pussy keyboard player whose gonna sit there like a cunt and plink-plonk away the whole night. No ..." I leaned in closer for effect. "You need *me*."

After that, the night shattered into alcohol induced blackouts, but when I woke up the next evening there was a message on my answer-phone from The Catsuits' management asking if I would be available to play with them on a probationary basis. I accepted, and Mark Brel's live appearances remained so sporadic that I managed to hold down the two jobs with relative ease.

As The Catsuits set off on our first U.S. tour, it seemed the world was at our feet. I lived in a Monkee's-on-coke dream world and even my parents, bless them, believed that I was famous. I think it was seeing me on the TV that did it. It was then that they finally stopped insisting that I get a real job.

The U.S. tour was brief but magically surreal. We had five days to ourselves in Los Angeles, and members of the group tried to outdo themselves with outrageous, boozed up, drugged out misbehaviour. The record label looked on and applauded, loving the controlled chaos of our youthful exuberance. I had just turned nineteen years old while the eldest member of the band was twenty-one. My adventure in LA started at a bar called Vida in Los Feliz with a young guy from our record label who was up for showing me a good time. It progressed to a three day pool party in one of Howard Hughes' old mansions in Brentwood, and by the time I crawled back to the hotel on the morning we were to fly to San Francisco, my epic crystal meth, coke, and lager rampage had taken me to Vegas, where in front of a small crowd of new friends who where almost as obliterated as I was, I married a girl named Christiane. As everyone told tales of sex and drugs during the brief flight, I sat and smiled. Then I dropped the bomb, flashing my gleaming wedding ring. Shock, disbelief, and then a begrudging respect made its way through my audience of band members, roadies, and record execs. Someone threw down a bindle of coke—one of the luxuries of hiring a private plane—and we cracked open a bottle of champagne to celebrate. I had set a record, we figured. It was one of the happiest moments of my life and I spent it with my best friends, my band mates for Christ's sake, on a plane headed towards a new city, a new adventure. This would never end, I thought gleefully, as we started to land and finished the coke.

That would be our final tour, as it happened. The Catsuits disintegrated under the weight of bad management, infighting, and Laura's increasing depression over our constant touring. In one of those moments of beautiful synchronicity, and in the same week the band fell apart, I found myself fired from Mark's group over a rumble in Moscow that had happened a month earlier. In one of the few public appearances Mark decided to make that year, the Mafia-organised run of shows in a prestigious theatre had fallen apart after an incident in a seedy nightclub. There, the honour of a pair of underage looking Russian whores was besmirched, a stripper dressed as Lenin was assaulted by a drunken Billy Idol look-alike, and myself and the tour manager received a beating for refusing to pay a bar tab run up by a head Mafia guy. While I was away on The Catsuits' final tour, I suddenly became the focus of recriminations over the incident which I could barely remember due to the amount of vodka I had consumed that night. I found myself out of two gigs at once. Before the end of the year, I was heading out of London with a couple of suitcases and a seething hatred for the record company machinations which had ended my dream in such a tasteless way and made litigants out of my friends. I was nineteen years old and I was going to LA, so fuck them! I wouldn't remain a has-been in London when I could make a fresh start in the city I had fallen in love with. I set across the Atlantic to reclaim my dream: I moved in with Christiane, my heart full of determination, and 3,000 dollars in my pocket. I knew I couldn't fail.

* * *

After being in LA for well over a year, I was still out of a record deal. Actually, my band getting a deal now seemed like a distant dream fading rapidly, and I was getting by on the old fallback—writing. I was messing around with an idea for a novel that never seemed to get anywhere. Since leaving London, I had been making ends meet by writing music reviews for a weekly newspaper and music video treatments for a handful of music video directors around town. It often paid very well, and in the first week of a good month I could have already earned enough to pay rent and cover living expenses. I suppose it was a testament to my laziness that even two hours of work a week started to irk me. I resented and couldn't stand to listen to the bands that I had to write about. For every piece of shit band that I cringed at on MTV there were a million others, each seemingly more mediocre than the last, who weren't even good enough to fool the mass of stupidity that is the American record buying public. I created numb-skulled video scenarios for New Country artists, middle-of-the-road rock bands fronted by men who looked like they should be chugging beers in some awful frat house in Hell, soft metal, funk, rap, even—God forgive me—ska revival groups. I tried in vain to block out anything but the paycheck from my mind. To make matters worse, there was the unfinished novel that sat by the bed, taunting me every night as I went to sleep, nearly two hundred pages of self-indulgent wank, which seemed like it would never be finished in any satisfactory way.

As I stopped work on the book and took on more and more work writing music videos, my sense of rage and impotence grew. My drinking and intake of drugs increased in indefinable increments at first, just as my relationship with Christiane started to fall apart at the same rate. It was hard to say where or when the rot started, but soon both of us were withdrawn and frustrated and full of mute anger for each other. Christiane was like some strange and alien form of life to someone like me, who had grown up in a depressed Northern English mill town. She had a life that I had only seen before in bad television. Her grandmother was a well-known Hollywood actress from the 40s and 50s and Christiane inherited some of that spoilt movie star sense of entitlement. She wasn't wealthy; her father snorted and drank away the family fortune before Christiane had made her teenage years, only stopping to find God and Alcoholics Anonymous when every single dollar and family heirloom had been sold, destroyed, or left as insurance against cocaine debts and bar tabs that would never be cleared. When I met her father, he was living in a shack on the outskirts of the city with a family of piss-stinking cats and a collection of firearms for company. He had once managed some of the biggest soul acts of the 1970s but he now had a crazed look about him, as if he had self-destructed before he could save his soul.

I was hanging out a lot with RP for a time—one of the endless list of people I knew on the fringes of the film industry —but when he found a steady girlfriend his appearances became ever more sporadic. I started hanging out with his friends, who became my friends to compensate. RP not being around as much did alleviate one problem—as my marriage stagnated, at least I didn't have to deal with RP's past with Christiane.

RP had a weird Midwestern cult family background. He landed in Los Angeles when he was twenty years old with long hair and a pretty, androgynous face. He went to work building sets, and then went to work on LA's drugs and women. Fifteen years on, he was still doing it. He built sets for the kind of movies that are only seen by people involved in the production of insomniac late-night cable viewers—dull, soft-porn thrillers, straight-to-video horror sequels, and vehicles for unknown rap artists. The films he worked on were almost exclusively directed by first-timers, hacks, and 70s pornographers on the skids. RP was older now, a little heavier, with his hair bleached and cut short, eyes perched owl-like behind a pair of Diesel glasses.

RP was also Christiane's ex-boyfriend. The photograph of her giggling underneath his draped arm on our apartment wall served as a constant reminder of that fact. His youthful and somewhat handsome face taunted me from various other photographs on our living room walls, staring at me with a James Dean sneer and a look in his eyes announcing ownership, superiority, masculinity. He was the only one of her exes that she still socialized with; the only one who she kept photographs of on our walls. When I questioned her about that, she would tell me that she only kept the picture because it had her mother / father / dog in it. He disgusted her now, she told me—he was a drug-addled asshole. The way she said it let me know, in no uncertain terms, that I, too, was in this category and rapidly falling out of favor. My jealousy grew in direct correlation with the stagnation of our sex life, which had started to disintegrate pretty soon after I came to LA over a year ago to live with her. By this point, our sex life had reached a virtual standstill; she constantly turned me down, throwing contemptuous looks when I laid a hand on her, making me feel self-conscious. After a while the looks became more than I could bear, so I stopped making any kind of advances whatsoever. Sex became a strange and rare occurrence in our home. This didn't really bother me too much. She had been fucking like a corpse for the last few months anyway, and had transformed with a frightening and baffling speed from the girl I met and married on a spur of a drunken moment, to an uptight, withdrawn stranger. She became expert in shaming me out of any kind of sexual demand. If we fucked, we certainly didn't kiss. She refused, point blank, to give me head. Towards the end, all I fantasized about doing with her mouth was punching the fucking thing.

I started to suffer from premature ejaculation, sparked partly by the fear of the belittling look I knew would follow if I came too soon. It was a horrifying look: at once emasculating, cold, yet almost sexy in a masochistic way. I told no one of what I was going through, since Christiane and I lived virtually separate social lives. It would have been too much to reveal the pathetic to my friends. When RP told me to watch myself, that she was an uptight ice queen, I had defended Christiane doggedly. But now my foolishness was being revealed to all. Me: reduced to a miserable, masturbatory shadow of my former self with my dear, dear wife—back turned, thighs pressed tightly together, less than a foot away from me physically, but still an ancient ocean apart from me. I suppose I had mourned the death of my marriage long before its actual end, coming to terms with the fact that Christiane and I were no longer in love.

It was the first time since I lost my virginity that I was so resolutely and unwillingly celibate. I had to find something else to pass the time and I sure as fuck wasn't finding it in writing. I was as uncreative as I was unsexual. Still, I had my friends, and I had my drugs. RP liked to go out and get high as often as I did, and I have to admit I got a self destructive kick from being around him, despite the whole grey area with Christiane and her possible feelings for him. Our drugs were coke and speed, and I soon discovered that he was good for finding narcotics at a moments notice. We would snort our way to the place where higher was not an option, days blending into nights and more days. And we talked—my God did we talk. It always came back to her: I remained silent despite RP's tales of their fucked up sex life, which (I noted with a little envy) seemed a little racier than ours, even before it had ground to a halt. He'd sometimes go to places that made me feel even shittier than I did before, but I

17

never, ever stopped him. Once back at home, I'd watch her sleep and meditate on images of him sodomizing her in the back of a truck. Everyone has a history, I'd reason, remembering the endless one-night stands I'd had on and off tour. I'd try and think of the girls I had lived with and slept with: Mette, the barmaid in Chelsea; Yuko, the singer and painter in Queens Park; and all of the others, an army of flesh fucked and groped in flats, hotel rooms, and bathrooms all over England. Then I'd think about Christiane sucking off RP while they worked on some dumb movie together. I wondered if she swallowed. I was almost glad we didn't kiss anymore.

"Fuck," I'd mutter to myself, climbing into bed. "What the fuck is wrong with me?"

Meanwhile, my relationship with RP was changing for the worse for other reasons. Since he found a new girlfriend, the chemistry changed slightly. He would disappear into the night to screw her as the Ecstasy or the coke or the whatever kicked in, leaving me at whichever party we had crashed to fend for myself. I suppose I didn't care too much; I actually felt relieved that he had a girlfriend. He talked less about Christiane now. I usually did okay when stranded—there was always someone with a car, high enough on Ecstasy to offer up a random act of kindness, or a house where I could crash on the couch. I was never in any hurry to make it home, to be greeted by Christiane with scorn or even worse, impassivity.

A WEEKEND BEGINS

RP called me on Friday afternoon to tell me that we were meeting at the Escape Room in Koreatown around ten. It sounded good to me; the Escape Room was a cool little dive bar, dark and replete with cheap cocktails and toilet stalls that locked from the inside.

It was around three p.m., and I was getting out of bed with a raging hangover. The night before I drank a forty-oz. bottle of Crazy Horse and ate four temazepam, trying to get somewhere on my book. It was a pretty pathetic attempt all around. I passed out around midnight and woke up still drunk at four a.m. with the words *This Book Is Shit* scrawled across several pages of my manuscript in a childlike hand. I crawled into bed, and Christiane left for work by eight that morning, failing to wake me up with her usual round of alarm clocks, stomping about on hardwood floors, and demands that I clean the house.

Despite my working from home, she treated me like an unemployed layabout. I know she secretly resented the fact that I made as much as her by writing for a couple of hours a day. When faced with my drunkenness and drug abuse, she cut down her drinking to borderline sober amounts. It seemed ridiculous, but I fought the sneaking suspicion that she did it just to spite me. Still, the drunker I stayed, the less likely I was to trigger another crying, name-calling, plate-smashing argument by asking her what the fuck was going on with us in the bedroom. I stayed drunk and high, and she tolerated my silence. I acted like a spineless asshole.

I didn't feel good. I realized I was going to puke, so I wandered into the bathroom and regurgitated violently into the toilet bowl. I called Joan, a pretty friend of RP and Sal Mackenzie's who had some vague managerial role over at

19

Nickelodeon. She presented herself as being well read, and she was definitely attractive. RP found her during a nine-day drunk nearly four months ago, and she quickly assimilated into our group. Dark hair and dark eyes, classically beautiful, I suppose. She had the look of a girl from a nice, middle-class family who had rebelled; her face had breeding about it, full lips, and smooth white skin. Nearly every male friend of mine was secretly (or not so secretly) attracted to her, and I think she knew it. Recently, I had sensed a growing closeness between us, and although I knew it was dangerous, I allowed it to continue. With the shit I had to endure at home, the attention of another woman made me feel slightly better about myself. I got through to her office first time—a rarity—and we talked casually for a while.

"You paying a visit to JB?" I asked after a few moments small talk, assuring myself that she was heading out with us tonight. JB was a friend of hers, a drug dealer who specialized in pharmaceuticals and Ecstasy.

"Sure."

"Will you pick up some stuff for me?"

"Yeah honey, what d'you want?"

"Couple of hits of Ex. Any kind, I don't really care."

Later, I wandered along Vermont for a while, picking up a copy of *Melody Maker* at Skylight Books, reading it as I ate at Orange BJ's, reflecting on the sad music scene in London. I was there when London was an exciting place to be: pretty boys in make-up fighting the glamour wars with their dour, northern, mop-topped opposites. And what was the headline now? "The Revival of Brit Pop?" Fucking hell, I remembered when Brit Pop was happening, and the phrase didn't sound so pretentious, so awkward. The idea of a Brit Pop revival seemed as tasteless as the chicken burrito that I was trying to force down in order to settle my stomach. Back at the house, I cracked open a can of Steel Reserve and I listened to David Bowie singing "Life on Mars."

Later that night, I was riding up and down Sunset with Daschel Tate, an oddball Hollywood agent who claimed to have psychic powers and drank alcohol as if it were spring water. He was a nice if sometimes temperamental guy, but he was about to turn psychotic through a lack of food. "My blood sugar level is plummeting," he warned me, staring wildly, "so don't fuck with me."

It was ten thirty on Friday night, just past Rampart, and he was insisting that we had to get food somewhere at least partly respectable, but the choices were becoming pretty limited this far east. When he told me he didn't want Mexican food I groaned, realizing that the search could go on forever and it was already getting fucking late.

After talking him into getting food at the Seven Seas, we drove back to his house with a six pack of Newcastle Brown, eating shrimp tacos. I was spewing a drunken monologue about the Ecstasy I took on Wednesday night, which was so cut with speed that I couldn't sleep until I passed out drunk the following night. We got back to Daschel's place, a spacious apartment off of Sunset and Benton, and listened to music while sucking down beers. Kraftwerk's "Trans Europe Express" turned the mood kind of odd, but the mad look was disappearing from Tate's eyes at least, so I knew that violence wouldn't be on the menu tonight. I cracked open my third beer of the half hour in his kitchen and looked at the picture of Napoleon mounted on the wall, as if it might offer a solution. I started getting antsy about the time—we were over an hour late to meet everyone at the Escape Room, and we hadn't even left the apartment—and Tate was complaining that he didn't feel like going out. I finished my beer in a gulp and told him that once we got there he would love it. Maybe my anxiety was making him feel worse, but I couldn't control it. I started to drink faster and faster in the hope of prompting him out of the house and back into his car. I was focused entirely on getting to the bar.

We took our last two beers out with us into the night, and Tate wasn't talking much as we drove towards Koreatown. We stuck to side streets; the car wasn't insured and we had open containers of alcohol ... not for long, though. With a long gulp my beer was gone. Soon after, so was Tate's and the bottles were tossed from the windows onto the roadside. Big band music and

50s New Orleans jazz played on the car's crackly AM radio.

The Escape Room was small and hidden away behind a strip mall. We pulled up at the nearby 7-11 and got out to use the ATM. Sitting by the machine was an older guy in a ratty suit and undershirt clinging onto a bottle of Mad Dog 20-20.

"Spare a dollar for a drink?" he asked, breathing death and decay up towards us on the desert night air. We got our money and walked into the waiting gloom of the Escape Room.

RP and his girlfriend were sitting in a booth, nursing Heinekens and laughing. Her name was Mya, and she was tall with large tits and a coal-black bob of hair like a 1920s flapper. She looked like a stripper; pretty, but in that fake Hollywood kind of way, with an animalistic sexuality about her. She sucked on a beer and licked her red lips in the same way I imagined she would before sucking RP's cock later in the night. A young cat called Francisco Engel who I had seen around from time to time was with them, glugging Vodka tonics like they were ice water and making drunken comments about the service a little too loudly. A Korean barmaid looked over at him with a sour expression as he laughed and looked away. A muzak version of "Smoke Gets in Your Eyes" played on the jukebox, and we greeted each other with "heys!" and hugs as we took our seats. Two whiskey and sodas arrived at the table for Tate and myself, and I disappeared off to the bathroom to take a hit of coke.

I unwrapped the bindle in the toilet stall, which smelled faintly of vomit and detergent, and spooned a little of the powder onto the end of my key, taking a blast twice in each nostril. Feeling good, I put it away, shivering slightly at the cold and the sensations beginning in my brain. When I got back, the others had arrived.

After a few more drinks and some more drugs, something in my brain switched up a gear. I passed my bindle of coke to Tate, then to RP who took me to the bathroom and cut out a couple of lines of crystal meth on the top of the toilet. We chatted for a little bit, uninterested and unfocussed before returning our attention to the drugs in front of us, snorting them and returning to the table. I was struck by an overwhelming sense of righteousness, that what we were doing was all that should be expected of us. I thought of Christiane, wondered where she was, and then pushed the thought out of my head.

Returning to the table, I found that a DJ friend of ours called Kris had arrived. He got a drink in and I asked him where Joan and the others where. Kris was a squat creature who was constantly pointing out to new people, at great length, that he had recently been in rehab for six months. He lied about the fact that he was in for coke, probably thinking it sounded too bourgeois, and said he was on heroin instead. As I watched him, beer in hand and undoubtedly high on Ecstasy, I couldn't figure out if he was full of shit or just stupid. It was Joan who had given me the low down on Kris's fantasies of being a junky, and it really soured my relationship with him. It made me consider him a fake and a phoney. Now it seemed every time he opened his mouth, I had to stop myself from rolling my eyes, just wanting him to fuck off. He was a second rate DJ too, playing bad, soulless techno. The whole fucking package, mediocrity and bullshit.

It was past eleven, and I really wanted to drop the Ecstasy before I got all fucked up on coke and speed. Kris told us that there was some party on Winnona and Hollywood and another friend of ours, Kat, was DJing there. They'd already stopped by to check it out, he told us, and we should head over there soon. Another whiskey and soda arrived at our table and Tate was starting to get drunk, ideas of staying in tonight slowly but surely disappearing from his mind. I took a mouthful of my watered-down drink and nodded hello to Kris, still talking about work with RP at our end of the table.

Pretty soon, we were heading out into the night again. I was reeling, kinda unsteady. I jumped into the car with Tate and offered him a bump which he hurriedly accepted before we sped off into the night in search of kicks. It was kind of ironic, since the party turned out to be right around the corner from where Christiane and I lived. We pulled into my parking space and as we were walking down Winnona to the house with its lights and groups of people standing drinking outside, I realized, even before we walked in, that it was going to be a bad scene. I remembered turning up there for a party once before with Kat and Sal Mackenzie, doing some bad speed and ending up paranoid and shaking in a downstairs room, unable to connect with the noise and chattering people around me. The house was forever cursed in my mind now. Plus it was nearly midnight and it didn't seem even half full from the outside. RP's car pulled up alongside myself and Tate as we were about to walk into the driveway.

"RP," I yelled. "This is going to be hell. Let's just pick up everyone, and get the fuck out, yeah?"

"Whatever," he said, parking by a fire hydrant in his big, old, white Chrysler.

Inside, we spotted them straight away. Sal Mackenzie and Joan were deep in conversation by the DJ booth in the half empty main room, and I realized that the party was even worse that I feared. Dotted around the huge, empty main room were coked-up forty something Hollywood scum laughing and high-fiving each other in Ralph Lauren suits. A survivor of the Sunset Strip glam metal scene staggered about with a bleach blonde perm and an open shirt looking like some ugly, awkward victim of evolution, a club-footed Dodo in leather trousers.

Sal, Tate, Joan, RP, Mya, myself, and Kris all met up and within seconds gravitated towards the bathroom. We were sharing blow and I handed cash over to Joan who dropped the two white pills in my hand. I smiled, gave a "bombs away," popped them in my mouth, and glug-glugged them down with a Corona I had found half full on top of the sink. I was hugging Joan and shaking Sal by the hand, asking him, "What's up?" Sal was dressed in his usual uniform of a well-cut, sober suit making him look like a 1940s bank manager. His appearance reminded me of Buddy Holly, and it was always a little strange to see his suited figure, with his thick-rimmed glasses and conservative air, snorting coke, dropping pills, or screwing underage-looking girls in the booths of bars. He divided his time between The Shop, a

24

repair joint that he lived above which never seemed to be open, and various strip clubs in and around Hollywood. He could be found every Tuesday night in Jumbo's Clown Room on Hollywood Boulevard, at the bar eating Thai food from across the road, drinking beers, and slapping the asses of the girls who were all on a first name basis with him. He often disappeared from LA on a moments notice to Thailand or Cambodia, and there were dark mutterings about what he got up to over there. Sal was a man without any kind of moral compass, and so long as you accepted him on this basis, he could never surprise you. It was best not to get mad if he screwed you on a drug deal or fucked your girlfriend while she was passed out drunk. He just didn't know any better.

The next destination was decided upon almost immediately: the White Horse Tavern on Western and Sunset. As the beer wasn't agreeing with me, I decided that it was time to switch to water or end up puking both doses of Ecstasy right back up again.

The drive was a blur, with Tate and me snorting the rest of my coke on the way over, pouring it into our thumb and forefingers, and sniffing it right up. By the time we hit our first red light, the package was empty and we were wired. We found a parking space right outside the bar and made our way in. Amazingly, RP, and Mya were already there with beers in their hands, and I began to wonder if we had fallen into a wormhole on the journey over here. Tate ordered the both of us whiskey and sodas before I could tell him I just wanted water. On the way, RP had acquired Dean Monaco, a lank-haired forty-something set dresser with a sardonic laugh and a sarcastic, dry sense of humour. I didn't get Dean, didn't know where he fit into the big picture. People seemed to like him, seemed to think he was funny. I personally thought he was a miserable asshole, and I treated him as such. He had been possessed by a bout of self-pity and depression for the past few months, and would tell no one where his sullen moods and self imposed isolation stemmed from. Because of this, his appearance tonight was even more of an unexpected displeasure. I took a gulp of my whiskey before I found myself in the bathroom with Monaco doing a line from the shelf, which conveniently circled the stall.

"We have to hang out more," I told him, almost vibrating from the effect of the coke, filled with a sudden good will towards Dean which wasn't really me. "I mean outside of this. We have to hang out more."

"I'm not afraid," he told me, snorting his line quickly and efficiently.

I gave up on my whiskey and ordered a glass of water at the bar. The barmaid, a full-figured, tattooed, Russian blonde with huge tits and a mean look in her eye, went to get it. Her boss, the old Russian lady, sat at the far end of the bar drinking Vodka 7's—watching, always watching. It was known about the place that she had an immediate distrust of blacks, tattoos, and men with long hair, fearing they were all drug addicts. A handgun was reportedly taped to the underside of the bar in case of trouble. Luckily, the old lady was usually too blind and drunk to notice the sea of drug deals and crime that flowed in every time the doors were opened.

We had taken over the jukebox and the Beastie Boys where blaring out, the bass line of "Brass Monkey" causing the floor to vibrate. The White Horse was huge, but nearly always empty enough to be cool. I hated waking up smelling of other people's cologne. As I received my water, the barmaid shot me a knowing glance which told me she knew I was fucked up on some kind of drug. As I made my way back to our booth I suddenly started feeling strange. It felt as if my head was expanding, and I had to catch my breath for a moment. Shaking, I made my way to the table and put the water down. The E had kicked in so suddenly and so intensely that I thought it would overwhelm me.

From somewhere, Joan and Sal had appeared with a bleached blonde manic depressive called Spencer who coupled bouts of inane overactivity with moods so deep and sudden that he looked as if he would be crushed by the weight of them. I looked at his pupils and saw the dilated black chasms of Ecstasy.

"Amazing shit huh?" I asked him. "It just came on walking over from the bar. Fucking mind bending."

26

"Hallelujah, brother," he grinned. "Bump?"

"Don't mind if I do."

And so the night continued.

As the first wave of the Ecstasy really started to hit, I hid in the bathroom looking at myself, the silence around me strange and alien. I whispered nonsense to myself, enjoying how it sounded reverberating off the tiled walls. My throat was dry and I was breathing heavily, staring at myself in the mirror, high as all fuck on the coke and the Ecstasy, the edge almost off the coke now, the pills taking over. I punched the mirror lightly and fixed myself in a stare again.

"Wa wa wa wa wa wa," I chanted quietly, enjoying the sounds it bounced off the tiles, and I fell out of the room and back into the bar.

"I have a concept about the human soul," I later told Joan, who nodded politely, high on speed, not coke, and seeing my highly artificial state of mind for what it was. "It is in the *middle*," I told her.

I was at the bar, watching the barmaid serve drinks to the drunken staggering clientele, raising her eyebrows and flashing her teeth at them, wiggling away in heels to get their beers and reaping the extra tips. She looked like a peroxided, 50s lingerie model, with a face sharpened by hardships, white fleshy thighs jiggling slightly as she clip-clopped about the place. RP told me that she also worked as a prostitute out of a Motel 7 room above the bar, and had done so for years.

"Come on, we're going," yelled Sal, grabbing me by the arm, and I realized it was approaching two a.m. I muttered "Where?" in a blissed out state, and someone said "The Wayward." Joan and her girlfriend Jo's house. We jokingly dubbed it "The Home for Wayward Women" one night, and the name stuck. Out we went into the night once more, shivering at the cold and the rushes from the Ecstasy and into the car, giggling like idiots, with Tate drunk on seven whiskeys and the beers we drank earlier.

THE WAYWARD

Tate was wearing a long black wig and I was laughing hysterically, both of us fucked up in Joan's bedroom while Donovan's "Season of the Witch" blasted from the Hi-Fi. Sal Mackenzie was cutting lines on the nightstand and Joan flopped around, coked up on the bed with Jo, a blonde costume designer from New Jersey who was tripping on mushrooms. I was dancing and RP had disappeared—completely unannounced—with his girl on the way to The Wayward. He was probably lying asleep against the warmth of her as we danced. It was four a.m. and all was well except for Tate, who took off the wig and said, "I have to go before I pass out." I decided to stay on, probably to crash on the settee when things started to wind down.

At five a.m. Sal pulled out a souvenir of his recent trip across the border to Mexico—morphine sulphate tablets. We all took the morphine and tried to settle down a little. Joan, Sal, Jo, and myself all lay on the bed counting the glow in the dark stars on the ceiling and bursting into unexplained giggles every so often. There was a pile of blow and a bag full of Ecstasy on the nightstand for us for whenever we woke up. Things gradually settled down, and I heard Sal's breathing become regular enough to indicate that he was asleep. Jo too, maybe. I figured the game was up, so I turned on my side and tried to drift off, but noticed that Joan was lying facing me, her large brown eyes as wide open as mine were. She gripped my hand in her small, cold fist and we lay there staring at each other for a while.

Eventually I softly asked, "Want to go downstairs and get fucked up?" and she nodded. I remembered being in this situation with her a month ago, when it was just myself, her, and Sal (again, unconscious) on the bed. I had tried to get her to come downstairs with me to fool around. It hadn't worked. She told me it "didn't feel right." The ghost of Christiane—beautiful, cold, untouchable Christiane who wouldn't sleep with me any more—hung heavy on us. Joan, though, seemed more understanding tonight. And she was undoubtedly beautiful.

We went downstairs to carry on snorting coke and speed. She cut out two more lines of crystal. In the background, I heard the pop pop pop that told me a record had ended. I walked over and took it off the turntable. I put on *Unknown Pleasures* by Joy Division. By the time the rhythmic and metallic thump of 'She's Lost Control' kicked in, we were kissing.

We started fooling around. I felt the hot flush of her breasts, her burning breath against my neck, the smell of her skin filling my nostrils. We froze with every creak and thump in the house, scared to be caught by Sal or Jo, inexplicably terrified of anyone discovering our attraction. I think she and Sal had some kind of thing, or maybe even she and Jo had fooled around—either way, it would be uncomfortable if anyone knew about us. I had almost fooled around with Jo once when I was fucked up ... it was bullshit. It was complicated.

And then there was Christiane, lying asleep and unsuspecting in our apartment.

Joan's cat, a mangy half-dead thing with falling-out, black fur suddenly pounced on the back of the couch we were sitting on and mewled loud enough to make us both jump and bang our teeth together painfully.

"We can't do this right now," I hissed, infuriated. "It's too risky."

"Yeah," she breathed, and although I was disappointed, I didn't feel too bad because I knew that it would happen now. It was inevitable. Tonight had proved that she now thought of me in the same terms that I had thought of her for weeks now. Months maybe. I had noticed a slight change in the way she looked at me over the last week, noticed that she held eye contact longer than was usual. There was a sudden desire to confide in me, to engage in whispered conversations away from everyone else.

We took the CD with the coke piled on it with us and we crept back up to the bedroom. We sneaked in and stopped dead. The room was empty.

"Where are they?" I whispered.

"I don't know."

Joan went over and put the upturned CD down on the nightstand, and I followed her over to the bed.

"Do you think they're in Jo's room?" I asked. She turned to me and shrugged, landing a light kiss on my lips.

"Do you think they're fucking?" I asked, and she sniggered.

"Probably."

She went over and locked the door. She walked over to me, smiled, and we kissed hard for a few moments, tongues twisting over each other, probing and exploring. I felt my hard-on rubbing against her thigh.

"Do you have condoms?" I asked.

"Uh huh," she nodded, and opened up her underwear drawer, pulling out a box. She undid my fly, freeing my cock, sinking to her knees.

Thud!

I look up, mortified. She turned her face away from the head of my cock as ...

Thud! Thud! Thudthudthud!

"Shit!" hissed Joan, standing up as I stuffed myself back into my jeans. She quickly handed me the CD—luckily with a rolled up bill still lying on it—and went over to the door. I kicked the box of condoms under a random pile of clutter as she unlocked it. It was Sal.

"The fucking door sticks," muttered Joan unconvincingly as he came in. "Want a line?"

"Yeah," Sal replied, "and let's get some breakfast."

We woke up Spencer who, as it turned out, had passed out on the floor in the downstairs bathroom. We drove to the farmer's market on Fairfax and Third around eight, getting a booth at Du

Par's for breakfast. Sal ran across the road to the liquor store to pick up a bottle of champagne. We ordered orange juice all around, and when Sal returned, poured them out into the spare glasses, topping up under the table with champagne. I coughed like mad as Sal popped the cork under table. Breakfast passed quickly. It seemed I was the only one whose appetite was sapped by the coke, but then I reasoned that myself and Joan were the only ones who hadn't slept. I felt physically drained, if not mentally. I scrunched my eyes, trying to wake myself up. Last weekend had degenerated into forty-eight hours without sleep, flitting from bar to club to house party, and I had managed just fine then. I'd gone out again a day later, and now, yawning in Du Par's I warned myself that any tiredness was just in my head. I was bigger than that.

"Listen," I said, "I have to stop by the house and email off some stuff to work."

"What are you writing, another music video?" asked Spencer.

"A treatment. For this band called Sugar Ray. They're fucking dreadful, and in the video they get blown up."

"Wishful thinking, huh?" snickered Sal.

We laughed, as Sal refilled our glasses with champagne.

We stopped by my house for a few moments on the way from the farmer's market—Christiane was at work and the house was clean and silent, so I sent off the treatment, cursing myself for not mailing it when I had completed it. Writing had been coming easy recently, and I had a few big artists actually turn concepts I had written into fully fledged music videos. The first single from Whitney Houston's new album boasted a video which sprung from one of my treatments. Still, there was something curiously unsatisfying about the whole process. I never got the opportunity to write for bands or artists that I respected. Although the money was great, I still found writing these things to be a constant source of bitterness for me. I tried to explain this to Christiane when she asked me what my problem was. I was hunched over the computer keyboard, listening to a Semisonic song that needed a treatment and cursing under my breath.

"What's your problem?" she sneered. "You wanna get a job at the Virgin Megastore instead?"

"This music is terrible," I hissed. "These assholes should be taken out and fucking shot."

"Oh yeah! You've got it tough, man. Somebody actually pays you to do this shit and you've got the balls to whine about it! Some of us have to work for our money, you know."

"It would just be nice," I told her, "to write for people I respected."

"You don't respect anyone!" she yelled, slamming a cup down, "and you know why? Because you're bitter! Because they're doing it for a living and you're writing their fucking videos! You're jealous!"

"Oh, fuck you," I told her. But she was right.

We drove back over to The Wayward, and when we stumbled out of Sal's big, black 1968 Ford, Kat was pulling up with Kris and some tall, skinny, blonde kid I didn't recognize.

Kat bounded over to me. "I've formed a new band and we're rehearsing in the garage right now," she announced. "It's a speed metal jazz band ... we're going to be called The Bitch Pussy Nigger Nazis. Do you want to be in it?"

"Sure," I said, bewildered, hugging her and introducing myself to her new guitarist.

"Jaz," he said as he took my hand, a scraggly blonde kid with high cheekbones and pale blue eyes. He looked like a hick, and so emaciated his skin was transparent, exposing nothing but sinew and bone underneath.

Kat was full of energy, bouncing around in a tight black top, her huge tits threatening to bust out at any moment. I had briefly formed another band with her, a punk band called The Hitler Sluts who played one gig at The Garage on Santa Monica before breaking up onstage. She played bass (badly) and sang a little. Thankfully, her ideas outweighed her talent. I hate talented musicians. Musicians with ideas though ... that's another story. I wondered absently if she was fucking Jaz.

Along with RP, Kat was probably my favourite person in the city, but I felt trapped, saddened by my own inability to express this in any meaningful way. Only at five o'clock in the morning, full of coke and booze and crystal meth, could we begin to articulate this to each other. The next day it just seemed like more drug talk and bullshit.

"Let's go to Jamba Juice!" she suggested and Kris grabbed me.

"Yeah come on. Let's get some juice."

Half out of my mind on cocaine and booze and sleep deprivation, the sudden whirlwind of activity swarming around me on the driveway became too much. I looked at Kris's idiotic, empty, grinning face and felt my muscles tighten. What the fuck was he so cheerful about all of the fucking time? Phoney asshole cocksucker. He was nothing but a useless West coast rich kid party boy, with his too-perfect teeth and Hollywood tan. I finally snapped in the face of his idiocy.

"What are you, a fucking hippy?" I yelled at him. "I fucking hate juice! Do I look like the sort of person who drinks juice? Fuck Jamba Juice! Fuck it and everyone who works and drinks there, fucking pseudo hippy assholes! Get inside and let's do a line, there's some Colt 45 in the fridge."

"Hey, its not even noon," laughed Kat, unsure of how serious this outburst was and hanging onto Jaz.

"And your point is?" I shot back at her.

"I love this guy!" laughed Kris a little too loudly, attempting to break the tension in the air. "He's crazy."

"I hate that word," I warned him before yelling in a mongoloid voice. "Look at me!! I'm *craaaaaa -zeeeee!!!!*"

I was left there, breathing heavily after my outburst, watching everyone dispersing, stunned into a momentary silence by my ranting. Shit, I needed a beer.

"That was kind of harsh," Joan told me after they'd fucked off to Jamba Juice, "with Kris, I mean."

"Nah" I said. "He knows I was joking."

"Where you?" she asked.

"No."

Sal laughed, and cut out lines for himself, Joan, Spencer, and I.

"Here's to Saturday night," he said, snorting his.

SATURDAY, JOAN, AND WHY I HATE THE ENGLISH IN LOS ANGELES

We hung out doing blow for the rest of the day, and when Kat, Jaz, and Kris returned with their goddamned fruit smoothies, Spencer disappeared into the garage with them to drum for their new band. Joan, Sal, and myself listened to the noise vibrating through the windows for a while before Joan announced she had to go to sleep soon. I went back to the Bike Repair Shop where Sal lived, and we carried on doing lines until seven in the evening, listening to The Stooges and David Bowie until I started to zone out. I started to wish that I'd slept.

The plan was to go to Spaceland to see a friend of Kat's DJ a set before trying to gate crash a party at Spot Studios on Santa Monica and Vine. It was a private party, and we had two tickets to sneak seven or eight people in with. I was watching TV when Sal shook me. The faces of the overfed, overtanned anchors on the news looked distorted and even more ridiculous than usual—hysterical and grotesque. I couldn't make sense of what they said, a garbled moron-monologue of celebrity gossip and idiotic punning between the soulless airbrushed newscasters. I almost missed the grey-clipped tones of British news. At least it didn't make you feel as if you were getting more stupid as you watched it.

It was Sal's hand on my shoulder and his voice saying, "Hey, its 9:30, we have to pick up Joan and Kris," which shook me out of my mental fog. I was momentarily confused, until I realized that I had fallen into a drugged half-sleep. I got to my feet unsteadily, muttering, "Let's fucking go. Let's do a line."

By the time Sal, Kris, Joan, and I made it to the club I thought I was dying; my eyes were heavy and I was feeling incredibly jumpy. The coke had fucked me up completely, and I realized that I had been doing lines now pretty much every fifteen minutes since nine o'clock last night. Now it was 10:30, and there was no way I could stop at this point. The more I heard about the party at The Spot, the less I wanted to go; the words "hardcore techno" were being tossed around, and I knew that the club had a 500-person capacity at most. I had an image of a small, dark, sweaty, hole with thundering dance beats blaring out of a maxed-out PA system, sweaty clubbers bouncing up against me, my coked-out exhaustion and paranoia reaching new heights of insanity. I began to fear the consequences of putting myself in that situation. A trip to the emergency room or a police precinct was definitely within the realm of possibility.

The more Kris started to hear about the party, the less sure he was that we could all sneak in on two tickets, even with Kat getting herself a ticket through some jungle DJ she knew. Somehow the party was transforming into the place to be in Los Angeles tonight. Kris and Sal's mobile phones started to ring incessantly after eight o'clock with friends and casual acquaintances trying to get hold of tickets. Of course, the idea of hardcore techno was pleasing to Kris, and he definitely wanted to go. Joan looked as doubtful about the whole thing as I felt, and Sal seemed as indifferent as ever. I was thinking we should dump Kris and head back to The Wayward to do more blow. I fucking hoped we would.

By 11:15, Joan and I were heading back to her house with the blow, and Sal and Kris were cruising over to The Spot. We arranged to meet up at the 3 Clubs at 1:30 to work our night out, and Joan and I decided to get a little more fucked up in the meantime. I was viewing everything through a haze of coke, Ecstasy, and sleep deprivation. We arrived back to the empty house and headed straight to her bedroom. I cut out four thick, long lines. I figured it was all I could do to even feel the effects. I handed her the CD, and she did her line, struggling to get it all up in one go. I watched her face wrinkle in discomfort as I turned on the CD player.

"Jesus Christ," she murmured.

She handed me the CD case and I did a line with the only

functioning nostril I had left. I snorted, chunks of coke going straight to my already numb throat. It was finally enough to make me feel the kind of burn I hadn't felt since my first line of the night. I had the taste of chemicals in my mouth, some song by Fatboy Slim blaring from the hi-fi, and the fire in my nostril creeping up into my skull.

As Joan started in on her second line, I began to feel bad. Real bad, real quick. A stabbing pain shot across my forehead. My stomach turned, I felt bile rising in my throat. I started shaking uncontrollably as I felt my body go cold.

"Put the coke down," I croaked, and as she did I fell back on the bed. My vision started to waver, making me feel seasick, so I closed my eyes hard. I could feel a bead of cold sweat making its way down my temple. I opened one eye cautiously.

"Are you okay?" she asked, suddenly concerned, leaning over me. So pretty ....

"It's fucked me. It's fucked me," I gurgled as way of an explanation.

"Shhh, it's okay. It's okay," she whispered, as she massaged my throbbing forehead with her cool, soft hands. I started to feel a little better. My stomach growled, ominously. She continued to work her fingers on my forehead, and I started to breathe slowly. My stomach growled again, weakly, after ten more minutes. My body was submitting. It was as if she had absorbed the bad feelings through her fingertips.

She leaned over and kissed me. My pager went off. Sal Mackenzie.

"Hey guys, it's me. It sucked at the party so I'm on my way to 3's, so either head on over or page me. Bye."

I cursed silently and broke the news to Joan. The thought of heading over to Hollywood and Vine to drink wasn't the most enticing of ideas, but I decided to let her make the call. She paged Sal back.

"Sal, it's us. Head on over to The Wayward, we're here. We had a bit of a situation here, but it's all right now. Bring everyone. Bye."

She walked over to the bed after hanging up the phone and sat down next to me.

"How long d'you think we have?" I asked, quietly.

"Long enough," she replied, handing me a condom and kissing me hard. We made love, missionary position. My gaze never left hers the whole time, and she talked to me in an excited whisper throughout. My hands mapped out her body, her breasts, her hips in the darkness, before we finished, dressed, and went downstairs without a word.

When the party restarted at The Wayward, I was completely out of it. We had cut the remaining line from earlier into four more lines to spread it out a bit more. I was trying and failing—throwing fuel into the fire now, feeding a psychological rather than physical need. I couldn't get high and I was slipping into another psychotic half-sleep that made me no use to anyone. Two English guys appeared with Sal, maybe half an hour after Joan and I had gotten dressed. One, a hulking skinhead, was ex-British Army who'd served time in Northern Ireland. He had that look about him—fat, sweaty face; alcoholic, watery eyes; awful tattoos featuring Union Jacks and bulldogs. I intrinsically mistrusted anyone who served in the British Army, finding the idea that anyone would volunteer to be stuck in a stinking filthy barracks with a bunch of other mentally challenged fools wearing itchy, ugly army fatigues absolutely shocking. Everyone I knew from childhood who went into the army was the kind of violent, bigoted moron that couldn't get a job sweeping the streets under normal circumstances. So they'd join the army instead, and some genius would give them a gun, teach them how to kill and send them into various political hot spots around the world. But upon hearing that these guys were army, I simply murmured, "Oh wow, that's cool," before staring off into the middle distance for the rest of the night. I suppose they seemed nice enough, but whenever I encounter the British abroad I try and keep my distance. They seem to feel that they are under attack from all forms of the new culture that surrounds them, and retreat into

40

bizarrely ultra-British caricatures of themselves. I know if these people wandered around Manchester with their flags waving and their soccer tops and their affected accents, people would think that they'd lost their fucking minds.

Sal left for the shop around three. Everyone but me and Joan was ready to keep the party going. The English guys, sensing that I wasn't up for a discussion about old Blighty, football, or politics, started laying into the lager and cocaine with gusto. I felt like a corpse, moving my eyes over to Joan every so often to see how she was doing before returning my stare to the wall again. My heart raced in my chest, and I was finding it hard to swallow. I felt like I had slipped completely into auto pilot, and I found myself reciting the words to my favourite songs in my head, trying to stop myself from going crazy.

"I'm going to bed," Joan eventually announced.

"Can I crash in your room?" I asked, a little too quickly. Even she looked startled by my desire to be away from the party.

"Sure," she shrugged, adding, "you can have the couch."

We somehow made it into her room and locked the door. I undressed and flopped onto the bed, half watching as Joan took off and folded her clothes. She slid between the sheets, huddling next to me.

"Goodnight," I murmured.

"Goodnight."

As fucked up as we were, we had sex three times before we finally slept, not waking until noon the next day. The last time we did it, we both lay on our sides and I fucked her from behind making small, careful movements. I hugged her throughout, burying my face into her shoulder. I briefly wondered if it was possible that I was falling in love with her. I thought that I probably was, although I had nothing to compare the experience to. Christiane flashed across my mind, but I blocked the thought out as soon as it surfaced. Over the past month she had become a ghostly figure, entering the apartment as I left it, leaving notes by the bed for me to clean the goddamn house, or coming in

41

drunk herself once in a while and shooting me dirty looks as I wrote, then staggering off into the bedroom to collapse unconscious.

"This isn't good," I thought as I came inside Joan, immediately starting to drift into a contented sleep. "This isn't good at all."

ALL THERE'S LEFT TO DO...

A week later I turned up to rehearse with Southpaw, only to discover that our rhythm guitar player Chris was no longer in the band. It was hardly a shock—he was constantly fucked up on heroin since playing a tour with LA psyche-rock band Electric Kool-Aid, a bunch of junkies notorious for turning on any and all of the people who drifted in and out of their circle. I had been exposed to junkies on the periphery of the music scene and had hung out with the heavily strung-out Atom, the lead singer from Electric Kool-Aid. I found them to be a pretty agreeable lot, a lot less annoying than stoners. Chris, though, became someone else on smack—high-strung, whiny, forgetful, and lazy. He turned up hours late to rehearsal, constantly tried to borrow money from the band, would stop a song halfway through to make obscure comments which made no sense to anybody but him. It was sad to watch. He had the hunted look of a man no longer in control of his life.

As I walked into the room, the first thing I noticed was the space where his amplifier should have been. James, our drummer, was setting up in the corner. He looked up, shrugged, and said, "And then there were four." That's when I knew.

The band's leader was Dito, a singer-songwriter from Astoria, Queens, who wrote impossibly beautiful songs about New York, innocence, death and most of all, love. He had the intensity of a man who had seen life and death in all of its terrible, close-up finality. When he turned up and we started playing, he said nothing about Chris. I figured he felt bad. I think we all did.

Afterwards, in the ramshackle waiting room up front, I drank a Dr Pepper while Dito fed a quarter into an arcade game. The rest of the band packed away and drifted off.

"Shame about Chris," I said, deciding to broach the subject.

"Yeah, yeah," Dito muttered wistfully, suddenly punching the Galaga machine as his ship blew up. Turning to me, "Wanna shoot some hoops?"

We walked out into the early evening heat and I ran across the street to a bodega to pick up a forty of Olde English, as Dito effortlessly dropped the ball into the basket.

That night, I was spilling out of the 3 Clubs with Sal Mackenzie and a Vietnamese kid called Sky who I met through a friend of RP's. I was drunk and tripping on a hit of E—not peaking too hardcore yet. I had just been doing coke in the back room with Sal and I was now sitting in the bar sweating, wide-eyed, semi-psychotic, rapping a bit with two kids from Texas who swaggered over trying to score coke as I smiled at them. Any other group of fuckers in there would have rolled them. They set themselves wide open for it, coming right out and trying to score off of us.

"How much d'you want?" I grinned, a sixty-dollar wrap in my back pocket, thinking I could maybe make a few bucks.

They said, "Oh, just a couple of eight balls," and I stopped, thinking maybe I'd misheard them. But the one closest to me shot me a wide, country-boy, shit-eating grin, and I figured that they seemed too stupid to not be genuine.

"Hold on," I muttered, and left them in the booth where they had interrupted me talking to a red haired model called Melissa. I had attempted to screw her a month or so ago, so high on coke I couldn't get hard, instead stuffing my limp cock into her soft wide cunt, somehow achieving a weak orgasm.

I tapped Sal on his shoulder. "Hey, is Oscar around?"

Sal turned, a pint of Boddingtons in hand and smiled. "Not had enough? It's a fucking Tuesday night, I'm holding a half. We're fine."

"Nah, these two hicks want to get a couple of eight balls."

"You know 'em?"

"Nah," I laughed, "they just strutted up to me and asked if I knew where they could score. The fuckers are lunatics, man."

"Take me to them."

I introduced Sal to the two jonesing kids and also to Melissa who I was rapidly getting bored talking to. She was pretty, not unlike Mia Farrow in *Rosemary's Baby*, but not very smart. The sting of my impotence was negated by the fact that when we had made it back to her apartment on Wiltshire she had been so fucked up on booze and barbiturates that I don't think she remembered too much of what happened. She worked as a waitress at some place on Sunset when she was between modelling jobs, and I was happy when Sal and her both split off with the Texans to score.

A few hours later, I was throwing back vodka tonics and laughing with Miro, a dominatrix from San Francisco who I had gone home with after playing a show with Southpaw at Goldfingers on Yucca and Cahuenga. I was standing at the bar in Goldfingers when I met her, just offstage after the set. The place was quieting down and I asked her if she'd like to get out of there and go get high with me. We smoked a lot of speed, and her permanently sweaty and pale boyfriend Pete walked in on us while she was sucking my cock. I was blind drunk—drunk enough not to be embarrassed, at least. But still, the fact that he walked straight past, made himself a sandwich, and flicked on the TV felt kind of weird. She started talking about a threesome with him. Somehow, the idea didn't really appeal. I took her to the bedroom and we fucked a couple of times in the gloom on her big overstuffed bed, stopping only to smoke more speed and take Polaroids. When I left the next morning, that was that.

"You are sooo cute, honey," she was saying while drunkenly caressing my ear, letting me know that if I was drunk or horny enough I could take her home again. I was distracted, though, craning my neck to see around the room in an attempt to catch a glimpse of Joan, who was meant to be turning up here anytime.

Lou Reed was blaring out of the sound system, and I staggered to my feet to get another drink. Suddenly, I thought I saw Joan standing by the DJ booth, and I approached her, tapping her shoulder.

45

"Hey, sweetheart," I said, but someone who was most definitely *not* Joan turned and smiled in an "I don't know who you are but I'm trying to be polite" kind of way, and she muttered back, "Hi honey." Over her shoulder, I spotted Sal talking to Oscar, a tall, black, coke dealer in a leather trench coat with a permanently affixed half grin. Sal was introducing the two Southern boys to him, and Oscar gave one of them a good-natured slap on the shoulder. I found myself absently muttering, "Oh, I'm okay," to the mystery girl before drifting away to the bar again. Soon the drinks where gone, and Sal was standing next to me.

"We've gotta blow. Pick up Joan and Spencer, head over to the Shop ..."

"You sort out the fucking Dukes of Hazzard over there?" I asked, about to nod towards them, instead looking round and realizing they'd already left.

"They've fucked off with Oscar, but he's dropping them off at the Shop so we can hang out a little, yeah?"

"Nice one."

I was shivering in the cold, piling into the old battered Ford with Sal and Sky and heading over to the Smog Cutter on Virgil where Joan and Spencer were drinking. Pretty soon we found ourselves ordering drinks from Sunshine, the crabby barmaid who constantly seemed one step away from drunken violence. I was hugging Joan hello by the jukebox.

In the bathroom I was doing key hits with her and Spencer, while outside a drunk Asian guy who looked at least seventy years old, crooned "roosy in the sky-hi wit dia-moonds" over the karaoke machine.

"Aren't you tired?" asked Spencer after taking his hit, sniffing a little.

"Why?"

"When was the last time you slept?"

"I caught a few hours on Sunday."

"So you've only slept a few hours since Friday morning?"

46

"Uh huh. So what? Sleep's boring."

Joan looked at me kind of funny, and something didn't feel right. I sensed her slipping away without explanation. It was almost inevitable, though, that our relationship would end in disappointment and unhappiness—it was created in such an atmosphere of chaos.

The sun came up and we were across town again in the cowboy's hotel room, rushing on cocaine and ecstasy, talking to RP on the balcony overlooking Western Avenue in Hollywood while the music and conversation fluttered about from inside like demented radio static. RP was asking me if I was okay—I suppose I was distracted that night—and I was trying to articulate the sense of inexplicable loss I was feeling, trying to find out for myself where the pain was coming from, trying desperately to second guess what would happen next.

"Where is this going to end?" I asked him.

"Death," he told me, "for all of us. For the whole city. The whole world, man. Can't you feel it? Can't you smell it? It's the last days of Rome, the empire is crumbling and we're doing all that there's left to do."

RP looked beautiful that morning. He had been awake for a couple of nights. His pupils were vast pools of night from the MDMA and his lips were dry from cocaine and crystal meth. He was dishevelled but in a deliberate way, and the early morning light gave a colour to his usual pallor. He made sense. He made all of the sense in the world, and there on that balcony full of whiskey and cocaine and ecstasy and speed I loved RP. I truly loved him as a brother, and I didn't want the moment to pass. I blurted out a garbled, "I love you," and immediately regretted it, full of embarrassment and inexplicable shame. But he reached out to me and put his hand on my shoulder and looked at me, telling me that he loved me too.

"I understand you," he told me, "don't ever doubt that. Don't ever forget this."

We came back into the room, and I felt better equipped to handle our reality than I had before. Maybe it was the drugs, but

47

I don't think so. Inside, Oscar sat on the bed talking to the cowboys, who sat in rapt attention at his feet.

"So I told this bitch, if you ain't got that damn money and you don't want your man taking a beating for this debt, you better figure out a way to work this shit off," and then he grabbed his crotch for emphasis. The cowboys giggled like schoolgirls.

"So what did she do?"

"What the hell d'you think she did?" roared Oscar. "That bitch worked that shit off, boy! Still ended up costin' me money. I'm too soft with those bitches. I ended up paying for an abortion for her, an' shit. She was a nice piece of ass, though."

IT'S NOT YOU IT'S ME

"It's not you, it's me."

I'm not sure if I had fucking imagined her saying it, or if she had in fact trotted out that particularly hurtful cliché. I can't really trust my recollection of events. I was still on the tail end of a drug binge, crazy with sleep deprivation. Joan had returned from San Francisco, that fucking town of overrated nightlife, hippies, and silicone valley yuppies breeding like cockroaches, and I dialed her number as soon as I heard she had gotten back. The weekend following our adventure with the Texans, she had left without telling me. It was near impossible to be home; Christiane, although totally unaware of my infidelity, was still freezing me out even worse than usual and the guilt ... oh fuck, the guilt. The irony was I was that I felt most guilty over my *lack* of guilt. I wanted to feel bad desperately, I wanted to feel something at least, but with Joan out of town I could not summon any kind of emotion whatsoever except loneliness. It just didn't feel like infidelity—Christiane and I hadn't fucked, Jesus, we hadn't even kissed since I slept with Joan. Who was I kidding? I hadn't so much as held hands with my wife for months prior to my affair.

I finally spoke to Joan two weeks after our last weekend together, and less than twelve hours after my last drug binge. In my increasingly desperate attempts to avoid the shit storm in my own home, I had spent the last two days with an alcoholic coke dealer named Mike who insisted on spooning more and more of the shit up my nose in between frantic freebasing sessions and blasting Rolling Stones tracks. He'd yell over the noise to me about this guitar part or that bass line, slipping into incoherent manias and trying to suck my cock when he'd get really high. "I'm not a faggot," he'd gurgle, red cheeked and sweaty with a

49

filth stained bathrobe hanging open, revealing the full horror of his spent and wasted body. "It's just a sex thing."

Time spent with Christiane was impossible. I slept there, nothing more. She had her work and her anti-anxiety pills, and I had ... this.

I gripped the phone hard, trying to visualize what Joan was really saying to me. I had felt a momentary tinge of jealousy when I discovered where they had gone. After spending the last seven days telling myself that it was okay to feel this way, that it was okay to miss someone like this despite being trapped in a marriage with someone I dreaded even seeing, I was ready to launch into the weekend with a new attitude. I was ready to tell her how I felt. But instead of speaking to Joan when I called the house on Friday, I spoke to Jo who informed me of Joan's unannounced trip with Sal, Kat, RP, and basically everyone I knew. It was my own fault, I rued. I had not been returning calls, not associating with my friends, too concerned with my piece-of-shit book which had advanced exactly zero pages and zero worthwhile words in the past few weeks. Christiane ghosted around me the whole time, tut-tutting and wondering aloud when I'd take up a day job to supplement my income. Eventually I snapped and screamed, "When we start fucking again!" and she got mad, smashing every dish in the house.

Now Joan was back. And she'd been thinking. About us. About how it could never work.

To save face, I agreed with her gamely. "I was about to call you to say the same thing," I lied, unconvincingly. And then for good measure I rambled on weakly about sex and friendship, inanely concluding that no sex was worth sacrificing a friendship for. ("This wasn't just sex!!! It wasn't just sex!!!" I wanted to scream when she fucking *agreed* with me.) Her relief was so tangible, so childlike and beautiful, that I even felt elated when I hung up the phone, relieved and overjoyed that I had done the so-called right thing. That feeling lasted less than an hour, and I later sank at last into a deep dark depression that threatened to swallow me whole.

Drinking coffee one morning with Kat, she told me how wonderful it was that Joan met someone as cool as B when she was up north, and how happy she seemed that he was coming down to visit her. I nearly choked on my drink, coughing uncontrollably and having to excuse myself.

Dean Monaco's birthday was the first night I met B, and by the time ten o'clock rolled around I had been doing coke and drinking with RP for the best part of a day. The party took place at the White Horse on Western, and we had taken the liberty of renting out a room in the Motel 8 situated above the bar so we could do drugs or carry on in any way we saw fit after two a.m. without having to relocate. RP and I spent the day driving round and buying beer and decorations to create within the small, damp-smelling room at least a tinge of party atmosphere. We settled on the cheapest theme we could find—hideous sixties smiley faces, (which were going cheap in balloon, table cloth, and mobile form)—and the room took on a rather sinister edge once every available surface had been covered. We bumped into Monaco on his way to a seedy Koreatown titty bar called Gold Diggers around one p.m., and he was already steaming drunk. When we rolled into the dark bar at ten-thirty he was almost catatonic on the settee by the electronic dartboard with a pretty friend of RP's from the East Coast, Lilly, who flopped over him in an Ecstasy haze.

Upon spotting B, I stared at him briefly, not trusting him enough to get too close. He was a strange new animal, which for the moment lay dormant, and I watched him closely. I honestly believed that if I got too close, he would take his chance and bite.

"I Wanna Be Your Dog" blasted out of the jukebox, and I drank beers saying "hi" to everyone who passed by, including a completely obliterated Francisco Engel who alternated screaming incoherently at his pretty blonde girlfriend and shaking my hand with a desperate urgency, staring at me hard and grinning, "We're the same, you and I. We're the fucking same, dig?" I nodded at the young, wild-haired drunk as he grinned and screamed, screamed and grinned.

I saw Joan from across the room and—determined not to exude any sense of weirdness—strode right over to her, kissed her cheek and asked how she was.

"Great," she replied, her pretty face lighting up as always when she smiled. "I'm doing great. This is B ..." and she motioned towards Him, his dark eyes burrowing into me. I felt weak, sickened in the presence of something bad and evil, impure and festering away in front of my very eyes. He was tall with light brown hair that stuck out at all angles from his head. His face had the sunken look of a man who had spend many nights awake while the drugs surged around his system. Tattoos covered both of his arms, stretched over the collar of his T-shirt and spelled messages across his knuckles.

"Hi," I croaked.

"Hi yourself," and he shook my hand, stretching out an arm and gripping my limp hand firmly. I wished a cancer on him as he did so. In my cocaine-fucked state I could almost see the hostility he was radiating towards me. It turned the small bar purple in a burst of heartache.

I drifted away, affording myself one last glance at her, and realized that the game was up. I couldn't entertain escapist fantasies of myself and Joan starting over, I would have to deal with the mess my life had become on my own. I turned away as they kissed. For a moment, I looked back at them and flinched when I noticed his eyes on me, his dripping tongue flicking over the flash of his teeth, dark eyes like a bird of prey about to make its kill, before he pulled away and returned to the conversation they held as a couple, slipping an arm around her waist. I overheard Kris telling some young girl, "And then I was in rehab for six months ...," as she stifled a yawn. I was fucked up on beer and coke, squatting next to a semi-catatonic Dean Monaco. He slowly and shakily brought another shot of tequila to his lips and muttered in a slurred and almost incoherent grumble about mortality, ageing and death. I smelled the onset of a midlife crisis in the semi-conscious drunkard. My mind was adrift, reeling; I was looking beyond him and absently staring at a pretty blonde who stood at the bar with a Corona in her hand talking to Sal Mackenzie. Then something that Monaco said snapped me back.

"We all have shit to deal with you know?" he was rambling, "and I don't know one fucking man in this bar whose problems don't stem from a woman. Not fucking one."

I grinned absently at this, as the girl who caught my interest shook her head at Sal, offended by a suggestion he had made. Monaco possessed an antiquated sense of misogyny, holding the belief that all men were powerless pawns against the castrating influence of female sexuality. I could definitely sense the generation gap between me and him; the two decades he had on me made most of his views and values seem embarrassing. But then he continued, "She broke my heart. She fucking broke my heart."

"Who?" I asked, almost interested. I wondered if he was talking about Lilly, who was dancing alone by the bar, but discounted this almost immediately. Surely the pretty blonde New Yorker would have never consented to sex with that shabby looking old fuck? His tequila breath drifted over to me, and I considered moving away when he suddenly barked:

"That bitch! That fucking *bitch* ... Joan!"

I froze and looked at him—all drunk, messy, and fucked up— in a place of such emotional hurt that he had lost any sense of dignity, spilling his guts to a near stranger who he must have known, deep down, did not give a shit about his crappy fucking love life. I followed his accusatory finger and watched Joan with her arms around B, and I could see the agenda now. They would leave early. Make some excuse, and then in the same room where we had secretly fucked, he would discover her too—undress her roughly, penetrate her hard, his hands traversing her nudity, their flesh intertwined. I looked at Dean. He had her long before I even touched her skin. I began to wonder if I was a fool, if I had mistaken my part of Joan's chain fuck of our friends for something that meant ... anything. In the face of a marriage that had left me feeling like an inadequate ass, I had set myself up for a fall that would leave me more alone and unwanted that ever. I closed my eyes and sighed, no longer sure of what was happening around me. I felt I was no longer in control, hurtling inevitably towards some kind of conclusion. The chaos of the past three months was nearing a resolution of some kind, whether I wanted to accept it or not.

Christiane showed up around midnight and demanded that I sit and talk with her. I shrugged, and she walked to the far side of the bar—the furthest possible point from where the party was happening—and sat down. I followed.

"So, how was your day?" she asked, sternly adding, "... day, weekend, whatever."

"Fine," I muttered. "I'm glad you came."

I was completely wired, finding it hard to focus on our stilted, awkward conversation, grinding my teeth like crazy. I looked over at the party, longingly.

She ordered a beer, I ordered a whiskey and soda, and we sank into a long silence.

"So," I asked eventually, "why are we sitting here? The party's over there."

"Those people are degenerates," she commented, smiling at me harshly. "I don't like any of them."

"Then why did you come?" I inquired, sipping my drink.

She turned and looked at me, and for a second we were almost back: two kids who thought they had fallen in love in four days, and committed to each other for life. That was just over a year ago. Now, she stared at me hard and said, "To be with *you*. That's why I came here," and I felt momentarily choked by sadness. I looked at my drink and then back at her.

"To be with you," she whispered, before standing up and walking out.

HERE COMES SUCCESS

I was lying on the couch, the uppers and downers and whatever else I snorted or ingested that night still flying around my bloodstream. It was maybe a week or so after Dean Monaco's birthday party, and my state of mind had been growing steadily worse. I felt spacey and sick from the drugs, and closing my eyes only caused odd hallucinations. Images of small insects or bacteria multiplying a thousandfold, intricate networks of piping which contorted and bulged with an organic energy, mathematical maps and figures—all variations on a theme, I guess, which had nothing to do with the normality I saw around me when I opened my eyes and observed the dying party. The smell of smoke, the taste of blood in my mouth and the pain in my bruised (possibly broken) knuckle, Iggy Pop monotoning, "Here comes success"–I felt worse than I had ever felt.

I looked around. Kris was still quietly trying to talk Kat into a state of unconsciousness while Sal lay on the floor already out cold. Tate, ever the realist, disappeared into the night when he realized that the party was winding down, a sixth sense that I sometimes wished I possessed. I got to my feet and made my way unsteadily to the kitchen. Thankfully it was empty ... what day was it? I had no idea, only a vague clue of what time it was, somewhere around close to eight in the morning. Eight in the morning at The Wayward, another drug and booze marathon. Jesus Christ, I was so fucking bored.

I sat on the linoleum cross-legged, my head thumping, and the beginnings of a painful hangover in the back of my skull. The urge to weep which had been torturing me since the birthday party all those days ago was getting stronger now. Light streamed in through the window and I felt like an absolute zero, having finally regressed to a point where I didn't care what happened next.

It's sad, but the whole affair with Joan and its repercussions made perfect sense; it was just another way for me to sabotage myself. I remember when I was seventeen, standing up on a table in a bar called The Three Bells—the table my podium, and the regulars my unwilling audience—and announcing that if I wasn't famous by the time I had reached twenty-five I would return to kill myself in that very bar. I was drunk and suddenly seized by the utter meaningless of my life in the north of England. I received sneers. Laughs. Someone, enraged by my cockiness, tried to throw an empty pint glass at me, but was stopped by their girlfriend. Looking back, I must have looked like an incredibly punchable young asshole.

"Do it now, son," someone yelled. "Give us a fuckin' laugh and save yourself some heartache."

I smiled, recalling the moment. I'd never have the balls to do it, to go through with my promise when the time comes. Worse than that, I wouldn't have enough honour to do it. How could I go through my whole life like I have, pissing opportunities up against walls, falling in love with the wrong people, failing to reach my goals, setting clumsy landmines for my marriage instead of having the sense to just get up and walk away, and yet then have the nerve to pull off a finale as beautiful and majestic and full of truth as that? A quick suicide would be beyond me. Better my life ended in the same way it proceeded ... slowly, and with no significance.

Finally, I was finished. I was finished with the party, I was finished with everything. I didn't need to say goodbye to anyone. I got up, and I got the fuck out.

On a whim, I called Chris. I hadn't seen him since he left the band. The last I had heard he was trying to get his burgeoning heroin habit under control. Without thinking, I called him and told him I was coming over to see him.

When he opened the door, he hardly seemed overwhelmed to see me. Hostility poured out of his large brown eyes in waves. He hadn't left the band on the best of terms, and I had been wary to speak to him during his own drug hell, which seemed to be spiralling even faster than mine.

"You look like shit," he told me.

"Thanks" I said, as he led me into the house. "I've not slept."

We sat around for a while, making small talk. He talked with enthusiasm about some new band he was playing with and told me he had a new girlfriend. I was ill and gripped by anxiety from the drugs in my system. I asked him if he had a beer. He told me that he was off booze for the time being. This surprised me a little, as I knew that Chris liked to drink as much as I did. I remembered the nights we had spent in the old days driving around LA trying to find parties to crash, open bars to drain. We were pretty close, once. Chris had always struck me as a little boy adrift in the world of adults. He was pretty, and girls tended to flock to him. Every time we played a gig with Southpaw, he would end up screwing the only pretty girl in the half empty club. At first I thought it was the fact that he looked a little like Keith Richards when he was at his handsomest, but later I came to think that maybe girls were attracted to the child in him. Despite his considerable prowess on the guitar and a string of model girlfriends, there was an insecurity to Chris that made him seek approval from the most mediocre of people. He would tell outrageous lies to impress even his best friends. At the time I suppose it irritated me, but in light of what happened to him there is part of me that wishes someone had been around to protect him from himself instead of egging him on into a habit.

"How about something a little stronger?" he asked, and I shrugged and said, "Sure."

We headed up to his room, where he locked the door as quietly as he could. He popped a CD into the player and went to his desk. He retrieved the tin foil and the heroin and laid it out on the bed.

I had smoked it once before, but had been turned off by the effects. It had made me tired and disinterested in all that was going on around me. I didn't get sick, but it wasn't the kind of high I was looking for. Now though, I thought that maybe it was.

I watched Chris as he cut a piece off the ball of black tar with a pocket knife and spread it onto a section of foil. He smoked quickly and with experience, following the bubbling melting blob of heroin down the foil with his pipe, inhaling the fumes and exhaling the smoke through his nose when he was done. He was in the process of passing me the pipe and the foil when he hesitated slightly and seemed momentarily in two minds about whether to give it to me.

"Look, we can go buy some more. I've got money," I said, thinking maybe that he was worried about leaving himself short.

"That's cool ..." he said, heavy lidded, "but are you sure you want this? You know the deal, right?"

"Yeah I know the deal," I told him. "And yeah—I'm sure."

I awkwardly smoked some of the heroin. I found moving the lighter in such a way as to push the heroin down the foil a difficult manoeuvre to execute while concentrating on following the drug with the pipe and inhaling at the same time. Eventually, seeing me waste good drugs became too much for Chris and he held the foil and the lighter for me, allowing me to inhale a couple of big lung fulls. We sat back listening to the stereo. Slowly, I felt my mood begin to brighten. It was unperceivable at first, but as I noticed a pleasant sensation starting in the base of my skull, sending shivers of pleasure throughout my body, I realized that I really didn't care about what was happening with Joan. She could fuck whomever she wanted. Suddenly, I felt silly for putting so much significance onto what was basically some coked-up sex between friends.

Even Christiane seemed like less of a problem. So it wasn't working between us. Either we could solve our problems, or we couldn't. It didn't seem worth making myself miserable for. I was twenty years old for Christ's sake, and I was worrying like an old man.

"Good shit, ain't it?" asked Chris, and I grunted in agreement.

"I love it," he continued. "Don't need to get drunk any more. Or do coke. It's nice not to wake up hung over and fucked up every morning. It's nice just to feel ..."

"Content?" I offered.

"Yeah," he agreed, "content."

As the shadows gathered in Hollywood we drove downtown to pick up more smack, buying from the street dealers at USA Donuts on Bonnie Brae. We pulled into the parking lot and stopped, sitting in a parking space with the engine running. I watched Chris, waiting for cues. There was a gaggle of ten or so young Latino kids hanging out by the donut shop and within a minute or so of us pulling up, one broke off and approached us. Chris rolled down his window as the kid who looked to be in his early twenties leaned in.

"Whatchoo need, man?"

"Chiva."

"How much?"

"Two twenties."

The money was handed over, and the kid spat out 2 balloons into his hand and passed them over to Chris. With that he was gone, a furtive look to the left and right, before rejoining his friends. I still felt great from the little bit of heroin I smoked earlier, and I took the balloon that Chris passed to me.

"Put it in your mouth," he told me, "until we get out of this fucking area. There's a lot of cops, man. If we get pulled, swallow."

GOODBYE CHRISTIANE

That night, Chris dropped me off back home around seven. I found the note on the living room table from Christiane telling me that it was over. She couldn't take me anymore. She couldn't take the booze and the drugs anymore. She wanted out, she was filing for divorce, and I was to leave the apartment. If I was looking for my manuscript, it was out back.

I opened the back door, and there it was; she had dumped it on the concrete steps leading to the parking space, covered it in lighter fluid and reduced it to ashes. It had mostly blown away into the evening but some pages remained, damaged but recognizable. I wondered if she read it. It had become something of a journal over recent months. It was all in there—Joan, the speed-induced sex with Miro, the failed attempt at sex with Melissa, the drugs, the way I had begun to hate her. It made sense, I suppose, that the book was the final straw.

I felt a vague sadness that the book had been destroyed. All I had now were older versions. Still, I had made no effort to hide the story from her. I left my ugly life in plain sight day after day. I suppose a part of me thought she would never read it, as she showed absolutely no interest in anything I did anymore. Then again, a part of me had wanted her to read it. It would mean that the truth would be out and the situation would resolve itself. A panic gripped me as I realized that what had happened here, by very definition, had to be final. There was no more pretending now. My relationship with Christiane, barring some kind of miracle, was over. Not that I believed in miracles.

I grabbed the note again and reread it. She was going to her friend Susan's place and would stay there tonight. She wanted me out by the time she returned tomorrow night. My shock receded a little and I started to get angry. I recalled every bit of hurt inflicted upon me, every stinging rejection. I wandered into the bedroom, and looked at the neat double bed with its grey sheets. The room looked like the rest of the apartment: bright, airy, practical. Christiane all over. I remembered going down on her here once, sometime towards the end. Sucking her clit in the dim bedroom, the first sexual contact she had allowed in a month or so. I stopped for a second, balancing myself on the bed and as I did so she looked down and hissed, "Keep sucking my *clit,* fucker! Jesus Christ, can't you do fucking anything right?" I stood up and grabbed the bedspread and yanked it off the bed, flipping her onto the wooden floor with a thud. And then she was on me, throwing punches and screaming curses, and I turned over the bedside cabinet, sending her trinkets and bullshit skittering across the floor. Then I grabbed her by the throat and tossed her back onto the bed. Standing over her yelling, "Fuck you, cunt!" stumbling into my jeans, storming out and walking shirtless and shoeless in a blind rage to the liquor store on the corner of Normandie and Hollywood.

Just thinking of it, I was gripped by that same rage again. I looked about the room for something to break, but seized by the utter futility of it, I went into the kitchen, grabbed a sheet of aluminium foil, and prepared to smoke some more junk.

That night, I walked to Bob's Frolic Room on Hollywood Boulevard to get wasted. On top of the heroin, the whiskey and sodas I ordered started to get me very drunk indeed. The barmaid knew me, and always made them seventy percent Makers Mark with just a splash of soda. I drank three quickly, and asked her to line up another. The bar was half empty. A couple of older Hollywood alcoholics sat nursing wine and beer, grey, spectral, broken-toothed, and huddled over the bar in the darkest corners they could find. Nobody talked tonight. The jukebox played Television's *Marquee Moon.*

A drink later she walked in. A young black girl, high on ecstasy … she danced across the room to Blondie's "Rip Her to Shreds," came over to me and leaned over my section of the bar, taking a long drink from my whiskey and soda. She was pretty with a wide mouth and a grin that exposed pink gums and gleaming white teeth. The symmetry of her face was ruined—just enough—by a scar which ran under her left eye. I called the bargirl over and ordered another Makers Mark and soda. I slid it over to the scarred girl and she accepted it, still without a word.

Later, back at the apartment, I screwed her on the bed, doubled over with her ass in the air. It was a hard, drunken fuck. We hung out in the house for a little, drinking malt liquor and passing a joint back and forth. She asked me about Christiane, whose picture was on the living room wall, but I didn't want to talk about it. We fucked again on the floor. At four a.m. she left and I started packing my things. I smoked more heroin, amazed by the sense of physical and mental peace it was granting me, before sleeping on our bed for the last time. The next day, I left. It was two weeks before my twenty-first birthday. The next time I saw Christiane was six months later to sign our dissolution of marriage papers.

It's hard to look back and rationalize how heroin became so important in my life during the weeks and months following these scenes. I suppose the first part is physical dependence. When you wake that very first time and you feel awful, like you have ice in your belly, like something is crawling around underneath your skin, and it's very easy to just react by throwing more smack on the foil and fixing yourself. I learned to barter away the future for a short-term bit of pain relief. And if I tried to make any concerted effort to stop smoking for a while, the reality of my situation would come back into focus and seem so completely fucked up that I soon went running back to the cocoon and relative peacefulness of heroin.

When does a habit become an addiction? When does the particular insanity that comes with choosing heroin as an aesthetic, as a lifestyle, become normal? I'm not sure; all I know is after a while of drifting along with things, of not dealing with my immediate problems and focusing instead on funding my heroin use, things shifted around me fundamentally. At some point I woke up out of heroin, and instead of becoming confronted by my living situation, my broken marriage, my precarious financial situation, I was instead absolutely sure that all of these things were No Longer Relevant to my existence. All that mattered was that I got some drugs to help me through the day. The other stuff, well, that was as abstract and distant as if it was happening to someone else. And in a way, I suppose it was.

GENESIS

It was 4:30 in the afternoon and I was at a hostess bar in
Koreatown scoring speed from Lori, a crazy, fat, meth-head who
worked behind the bar and doled out grams of crystal for sixty
dollars a pop to tweakers and all kinds of crazies who came from
as far west as Hollywood to cop. The place had a stench of cheap
aftershave which lingered in the stale air, with old Korean
businessmen sitting around Formica tables nursing overpriced,
watered-down whiskey and the thunk-thunk of chunky thighs as
plump, gone-to-seed blonde girls sashayed from table to table
looking for business. It was the girls' jobs to entertain the men,
bring them drinks, laugh at their jokes, run their hands through
their hair. The more the men paid, the more they got. The best
money always went to the white girls with blonde hair, and even
the most beaten up and drug-fucked of them made twice as much
as the Asian girls. Lori, always wired but never any thinner, shot
me a grin full of broken, ground-down tweaker teeth and slid two
grams wrapped in a napkin across the bar to me.

The place was half-empty and the constant gloom made me
feel as if it was midnight and not a blazing desert afternoon. The
only light was the neon screaming *"Ice Cold Beers–Cocktails"* and
the almost luminescent pallor of Lori's skin. I was about to leave
when a familiar figure pulled up a stool next to mine, and
slumped forwards over the bar. I recognized her as Genesis, the
girlfriend of a kid I saw from time to time named Bobby. She was
from the Midwest: pretty, with a heart-shaped face, blonde hair,
and pale blue eyes. She looked tired though, older and thinner
since I last saw her.

"Hi, stranger," I said, causing her to look up and blink her
teary eyes in recognition. "What's wrong?"

"Oh," she sniffed, wiping her eyes with a tiny pale hand,

"n-nothin'." I just split with Bobby and I'm crashing. Haven't slept in a while."

Lori was at the other end of the bar sliding drinks over to a waitress with two blue tears inked on her cheek, who silently chewed gum and stared at the ceiling fan.

"Wanna get high?" I asked Genesis, her face lighting up at the very words. "I'm holding..."

I took her to my car. Los Angeles being Los Angeles, one of the first things I had to do after being kicked out by Christiane was buy a car. I am no car lover, so I bought the ugliest, cheapest, most un-LA car I could find—a 300-dollar, reconditioned, eggshell blue Volvo with rust patches and an engine that gave out frequently.

Driving back to my apartment on Iris Circle, she filled me in on what had been happening. She was still working at a hostess bar not far from Lori's and had been supporting Bobby while he worked on his music, paying for all of the drugs. When they started doing more and more speed, she needed to make more money, and Bobby started getting uptight that she was staying over with guys who came into the bar and attending "parties" organized by the club for some of the better paying clients.

"Its bread man, that's what I told him. What are you gonna do? So I gotta screw some old Chinese fuck, no big deal right? But he gets all possessive, and slaps me around ... fucking asshole. He's still happy to shoot the crank my pussy pays for, though. So I left him."

I had been at my new apartment for three months, but it was still filled with nothing but a TV, my CD Walkman and empty take out containers. When we got there, she walked around, sizing up the room, running her hands along the work surfaces.

"Nice place," she commented. "Lots of room."

We sat down on the floor cross-legged, and I threw the baggie of speed down between us. I took out the glass pipe and watched as she pulled out a Hello Kitty pencil case from her purse and popped it open, exposing a needle in its plastic wrapping and a rubber tourniquet.

"You got a spoon?"

"Sure."

She poured a little speed into the spoon, added water and swirled it around. Then she took out a packet of Marlboro's, ripped the filter off the end of one, and dropped it into the solution. The needle was taken out of the packaging, the liquid drawn up into it before she rolled up her sleeve and tied the tourniquet around her arm. I stopped what I was doing to watch, fascinated, but she was so wrapped up in her ritual that she didn't seem to notice. She slid the needle into the crook of her arm and almost immediately a red-black glob of blood flowered in the clear solution. She snapped the tourniquet off with her teeth and pushed the hit home.

She withdrew the needle, wiped the spot of blood from her arm and closed her eyes.

"Oh thank fuck ..." she exhaled, "that is sooo good. Thanks, baby."

It was different to how I imagined shooting up to be. The needle was much smaller than I'd expected, and it didn't seem very messy at all. Not all blood and guts, quite painless and sterile.

"How does it feel when you shoot it?" I asked her, placing my pipe back on the floor still unloaded.

"Great. Totally different from smoking or snorting it ... just ... incredible, I guess. Like how diving out of a plane would feel. I feel so ... *great* right now."

"You got a spare needle?"

"Yeah, sure. I always come prepared, honey."

"Will you shoot me?"

"Sure, why not?"

I watched, stomach turning in excitement and fear as she prepared a shot in the exact same way. I tied the tourniquet around my own arm, flexing while she ripped open a new syringe and drew up the hit. I watched as she slid the needle in, telling me that I had good, fresh veins, watching my own blood fill the dropper so dark and thick, looking almost like the contents of a biological lava lamp in the barrel of the needle. She snapped the tourniquet off with one hand, keeping the needle steady in my arm with the other, and then slowly fed the shot into me. I imagined that I could feel it going in, that it felt cold, and it wasn't until it was all in and she started to withdraw the needle that I sensed it starting, something building in the base of my skull and my stomach, my heart starting to beat faster as waves of euphoria and nausea tore through me almost so strong that they overwhelmed me. Genesis watched me, smiling, as my eyes registered shock at the intensity of the hit, so different from anything I had ever felt before, a kind of whole body vibration, the kind of hit I had always wanted but never gotten completely from a drug. She told me to keep breathing and go with it, her voice distant and tinny, almost lost in the roar of my blood rushing in my ears. In a few moments the most intense flash of pleasure and fear was over and my body settled down somewhat, still buzzing and pinging with the intensity of the methamphetamine, and I lay back on the floor muttering, "Oh god, that feels so fucking good," and we both lay there giggling and laughing, before—like ballet—we undressed without acknowledging it, and fucked in that brutal, endless crystal meth way, cock and pussy hammering against each other, yelling and rolling about on the floor, not coming but just stopping in an exhausted heap before shooting up again.

That afternoon developed into a two-day speed and heroin run. We cooked up some of my black tar heroin from MacArthur Park next, and I was hit with my second revelation: the beautiful intensity of heroin pushed home into the mainline. The gentle euphoria and disconnected peace of mind of the drug was multiplied tenfold, combined with a rush which felt like my muscles were turning into warm honey and drip-dripping down my spine and into my feet.

I knew somewhere in the back of mind that I had turned a corner from which it would be very hard to come back, but when you've got heroin it just doesn't matter. Genesis stayed with me, coming back the following night with all of her belongings in four bags. She set up camp in the front room. It was great for the first few weeks; she brought me down to a storefront needle exchange on Cahuenga and Hollywood where you could buy 100 clean syringes for ten dollars (or a donation of less if you were broke), and we hung out together getting high and fucking.

After a few weeks we were just getting high. She would take off for days at a time to work and would come back with a couple of hundred dollars, sometimes more, bitching about the way this one stank, or that one kept trying to stick it in her ass without lube. Everything was always okay, though, when she was back at the apartment and had her drugs around her.

The honeymoon lasted for a month or so. I suppose we were fatally mismatched from the beginning because at the end of the day, she was a speed freak and I was more naturally inclined towards heroin. I couldn't take speed for more than a few days at a time; the nightmarish comedown and depression that followed coupled with the hallucinations caused by lack of sleep all eventually drove me crazy. After the first twenty-four hours, I started to obsess, repeatedly checking that the door was still locked, or that the cops were not outside … sometimes I would become convinced that ants were swarming over all of the white surfaces in the kitchen, only for them to vanish when I reached out to touch them. As soon as I moved away, out of the corner of my eye, there the bastards were again.

Genesis frequently expressed a fear of doing too much heroin because she didn't want to become strung out. I asked her what the big deal was, repeating what I had heard from Chris, that coming off of heroin was no worse than having the flu for a week. She asked me if I had ever stopped completely since I started all those months ago and I told her that I hadn't. She nodded at this, as if to say, "Well, just you wait." I would retaliate by asking her when the last time was that she went a week without shooting speed, and she would try and fail to remember. She said it had been a year at least. I then would nod, thinking, "touché," as I prepared a shot of heroin for myself.

NEAR MISSES (Part One)

"Oh fuck. Oh fuck oh fuck oh fuck. Fuck SHIT man!"

That was Chris, who had become my partner over the last weeks on our regular trips to score off the street. Up until now we had been on a typical, uneventful drug hunt. There is nothing like scoring heroin off the street to make you feel dirtier and more used up than you already are. A fat Mexican sticking his head through the passenger side repeating, "Whatyouwan, man? Whatyouwan?" until you cough out, "Chiva" and thrust the bills towards him. Then him spitting out the tiny balloons into your hand and you stashing the saliva soaked objects under your own tongue as you drive away. Yeah, it makes you feel real good about yourself, but you don't care. You Have the Drugs. And then, oh Christ, the night is looking up already.

Pulling out of Bonnie Brae and onto 6th, our uneventful night suddenly turned eventful. The street was a notorious haunt for heroin dealers, and as we circled the parking lot outside of USA Donuts I began to feel a little uncomfortable at the lack of action in the area. Something was in the air. Something had scared the dealers and the other junkies away.

Chris was muttering something about Mexicans as he pulled out onto 6th and headed west, and I was the first to notice the black and white patrol car tailing us almost immediately. After a block and a half, they began to flash the brights.

"Oh fuck," the kid muttered, "oh fuck oh fuck oh fuck! Fuck SHIT man."

"Pull over," I ordered, "and chill the fuck out, okay? Do you have drugs on you?"

"No," he said, shaking, pulling over.

"Anything. Blow? Anything?"

"No."

"Good. Be cool then."

"Step out of the car," a cop instructed. "Driver first."

Chris made his way out, stood against the wall and spread his legs.

"Now you."

The second cop frisked me and I looked over absently at Chris as he emptied his pockets. The cop's hand rested lightly against my chest for a moment.

"Why you so nervous?" he inquired, trying to deceive me with his nonchalant tone.

"I've never been stopped by the police before," I replied, trying to keep my voice neutral and flat sounding.

"I know you guys were trying to buy dope," the cop tells me later as his partner turns the car over. "Why don't you make it easy on yourself and 'fess up?"

I looked blank, not avoiding eye contact but keeping a poker face.

"No. We got lost. We were just turning around. We don't have dope; we didn't try to buy dope."

In the end, we lucked out. They didn't feel like fucking with us I guess, so no trip downtown, no cavity search, nothing. Just a warning and a reprieve. Driving back to Chris's house, he was shaking and quiet. I had already decided to try and give dope a break, when suddenly he turned around and said, "Maybe we could get some crack instead. I know a place," as we hit Western.

GIMMIE SHELTER

"You need to get out of LA for a while, man."

I had heard it from a few of my friends in various situations for a couple of weeks. I wasn't looking so good, and I suppose I seemed a little down. I didn't want to go to the parties anymore, I didn't want to drop Ecstasy or snort coke. I wasn't interested in getting laid. A few of them thought I had taken the break-up with Christiane harder than expected; others suspected Joan was the cause of my change in behaviour. They all could not have been further from the truth. RP spotted a bruise on my arm and gave me a suspicious look. I stared right back at him; in an unspoken moment he became the first of our friends to know that I was injecting. To his credit he never gave me a speech about it—he was too much of an unrepentant hedonist to ever try and pull that kind of patronizing bullshit. No, RP was good people; he just said, "You know; you should get out of LA for a while, man. You need a break."

"I'm leaving tomorrow," I told him, "for a few days. I've got some work in Laughlin with a film crew."

"Good, man. Take it easy. We'll have some beers and a few lines when you get back."

Laughlin, Nevada. The poor man's Vegas, or the Vegas of the future depending on who you're talking to. Laughlin had none of the glitz and pretence of Vegas, and it didn't try to cater to families and fat hicks from the Midwest like Vegas did. Laughlin was a town for gambling, and if you didn't like gambling, and you were in Laughlin ... well, you were pretty much fucked all around.

The gig came about in the most convoluted and spurious of ways, but let's just say I agreed to something when I was drunk at a party with some friends of a friend, and the bastards remembered my phone number and called me up to see if I'd be interested in working on a low- budget documentary to be shot in Laughlin.

"What's the documentary about?" I asked the kid on the phone.

"Tribute bands. Get this; we're filming a Rolling Stones tribute band playing in a casino, which will be hosting the annual Hell's Angels River Run. Whaddya think?"

With my friend's words ringing in my ears, I accepted. Three days later I was in a van, and Genesis was on her own in my apartment for a couple of nights.

My plan was to use the trip to cut down my heroin intake to a marginal level, maybe even kick altogether, and get paid to do it. There wasn't a particular reason that I wanted to stop, just the usual, nagging, three-in-the-morning doubts that the longer I did this, the harder it would be to stop. It was costing me more and more money to get high as my habit increased. I figured I needed a break, if only for a week or two, so I could get stoned on less dope again. I was pretty early on in my habit so I figured that kicking would be a breeze. I just needed some meaningful activity to keep my mind off of dope, and what better activity than helping make a documentary on the "legendary" Stones tribute band The Really Stoned?

I left LA in a minivan with the filmmaker, a scrubbed-up, healthy college boy called Sam who was way too cheery for my liking, (and whom I later became convinced was slightly retarded), a stoner sound guy called Paulie who wore a filthy Megadeth T-shirt which left his pale flabby gut hanging exposed, and the camera guy Jules, who acted like he had never so much as handled a video camera in his life before making this movie and who constantly muttered incomprehensible complaints to himself like, "... hmmmm, we're losing the light for the tripod boom set-up, you know, the long shot, hmmmm ..."

And of course there was the band.

The band themselves were the most ludicrous and motley collection of fags, mooches, wash-ups, and has-beens it has ever been my misfortune to encounter. The stink of desperation and

74

failure hung around them as if they had been sprayed by some terrible, vengeful skunk. The guy who was meant to be Mick Jagger looked like an overweight drag queen trying to pass for butch and failing, while the rest of the band was a bunch of alcoholic session guys from the 70s who had been dragged out of semi-retirement in the Valley and stuck into ill-fitting velvet jackets and fright wigs in the vain hope of passing them off as being at least in their mid-thirties. The one who was trying to be Keith Richards was either talking with the worst, most affected British accent I have ever heard, or had an unusual cleft palate which made him sound like John Merrick meets Dick Van Dyke.

"Yooo fink dere'll be chickies dere?" he was asking.

"Oh, I'd be careful," Sam piped up. "I don't think the Angels appreciate people messing with their women."

Keith Richards nodded sagely and I stifled a groan, thinking that he should be more worried about undercover cops—the only action that old fuck was gonna see in Laughlin was the type that charges twenty bucks for head. As we all left Los Angles I asked, "So where are we sleeping? In the casino or a Holiday Inn?"

Everybody laughed a little.

"Oh no," said Sam, "no money for that, I'm afraid. We're going to be sleeping in the van. The band is staying with some friends in town. We can use the bathroom facilities at the casino, though. That's not a problem, is it?"

"Oh no," I said. "No problem at all. That's just ... great."

That was the point where I realized my attempt to cut down or quit heroin would have to happen another time. In fact, I decided, I would need more heroin than I already had. I would need to find a connection in Laughlin as a matter of urgency.

"You need to get out of LA ..."

Yeah *right*, fuckers.

* * *

Laughlin reared out of the desert like impending doom, not even a poor man's Vegas—more like a poor man's Atlantic City or Reno. We pulled up at Harrah's Casino, where the annual Hell's Angels River Run was hosted, to an awesome sight. It was late afternoon and the desert sun was reflecting off of a sea of chrome; bikes stretched out as far as the eye could see in every direction, swamping the parking lot and the entrance to the hotel in a fuel-belching mass that created a roaring sound akin to that of the fabric of the universe being ripped apart. Everyone was awed into silence by the noise and the mass of hogs. A scrolling neon sign announced, "Laughlin Welcomes Hell's Angels," in ten-foot high gold letters.

"Well, this should be interesting," commented Charlie Watts.

"Let's get to the house," Mick Jagger interjected. "I need to take a dump."

We circled around the lot and I saw the men standing around the bikes, drinking beers and laughing, slapping their buddies on the backs, all faded denim and leather vests with insignias of their chapters ... and of course the Angels' logo. They had handlebar moustaches and aviator shades; late thirties, big-titted, blonde girlfriends who lifted up their shirts when anyone whistled at them or when a new hog roared past, exposing their swollen, surgically enhanced tits to approving roars and whoops. I was struck by the absurdity of it all, still amazed that the Hell's Angels really existed out of the movies or books by Hunter S. Thomson. They seemed like a quaint throwback to a different age, an age without the Internet or instant celebrities or reality TV. Yet here they were, smoking and burping and slapping asses in this backwater gambling town on the Colorado River as ugly and as large as life itself.

As we pulled away and headed to the house where the band would be staying, I suddenly started to become very afraid of leaving Los Angeles for this madhouse, even for a few days. I had nothing here; I was a lost and stupid English drug addict with no possible way to comprehend what was happening around me. I felt sure I would live to regret my decision to leave LA.

As nightfall descended, I was in a taxi headed back to the strip. Everyone else was at the house, which turned out be owned by two drunken Valium-addicted ex-strippers who, of course, were "deeeeaaarrr friendsshh" of the band. Maybe in their booze and diazepam haze, they really thought these people were the Rolling Stones. Maybe they even thought it was still 1967. Who could say?

A party droned on with bottles of Jack Daniels and crappy soft rock music, when I made my excuses and called a cab. The house was tiny and smelled of cats, hidden up in the hills with what seemed like no other living things for miles around. Looking out at the dust and the vast nothingness, it seemed as if I could have been dropped on the moon with this collection of students, stoners, crazies, and freaks. Cooking up a shot in the bathroom, (replete with topless pictures of our hosts obviously taken sometime in the early 70s and a mound of cat shit in the corner), I was repeatedly interrupted by one of these swaying and slurring car wrecks who beat on the door and yelled, "Ohhhh honey, how long ya gonna be in there? I gotta pee *reeeeaaallll baaaaad.*" I fucked up the shot, blew out a vein in my goddamned wrist in a burning explosion of pain, and only felt half the effect that I should have.

Still, in the cab going into town, the motion of the car started to lull me into a nice stoned nod and I started to feel the familiar excitement of going to score.

"So where are we going, sir," the cabbie asked cheerfully. "One of the casinos?"

"No," I told him, "bring me to the worst part of town."

The driver was taken aback. He paused for a moment and asked me to repeat myself.

"The worst part of town, man. You know what I'm taking about. Drug dealers, prostitutes … that kind of thing."

He started to get all coy on me, talking about how he didn't know much about "that kind of thing" and how Laughlin is a quiet town. I dangled ten dollars through the partition and laid it out country simple for him.

"Look, you're a cab driver. You know this place, I do not. I am in desperate need of someone who is gonna sell me some drugs. Hard drugs. I ain't a tourist; I got no interest in gambling or seeing the sights. What I need is to be dropped off in the kind of place where I might find that kind of action. Can you help me?"

The driver paused for a second and took the bill before driving the rest of the way in silence, allowing me to enjoy the remnants of my shot in peace.

He dropped me off at a seedy looking strip mall across from a broken down motel, well away from the casinos and neon lights. A few sad looking streetwalkers, overweight and dressed like they were heading to the Stop and Shop, drifted around the place. There was a check cashing joint and a pawn shop still open, and a gloomy looking bar called *Casanovas*. I paid the driver and he took off without a word. I figured I should head to the bar to get straight.

Inside, the air of dilapidation and decay was even stronger than outside. A sad looking Christmas tree and neon Santa Claus tried their best to create a festive spirit, despite it being late April. The place smelled of sweat and stale cigarette smoke, and an infomercial for diet pills bleating out of a small black and white television behind the bar created the only soundtrack.

I walked up to the bar and ordered a beer. The woman behind the bar was an older, dark-skinned Native American. She said nothing to me but, "three dollars." I handed her the money. She returned to the far end of the bar and picked up her cigarette right where she left off.

The beer tasted flat and stale but I persevered with it while taking in the rest of the bar. A pool table sat unused. A fat guy in a cowboy hat pushed coins into the cigarette machine, and a woman sat alone in a booth nursing a drink. I took in her face: the sucked-in cheeks, the dirty blonde hair tied back in a severe looking bun, the glazed eyes … she could have been anywhere from forty to seventy years old. There was no doubt in my mind this woman was a junky, so I got up and walked over to her.

"Do you mind if I sit?" I asked her, and she looked up and

raised an eyebrow.

"Sure," she said, as I slid in next to her.

"I haven't seen you in here before," she murmured. "You from the neighbourhood?"

"No, I'm visiting from LA."

"Well," she grinned, taking a long gulp from her drink, "You sure as shit ain't sightseeing in this place. Lemme guess, you're looking for something, right?"

"Maybe. You know where I should go to get it?"

She leaned in conspiratorially.

"You looking to score rocks?"

"I'm looking for heroin."

She leaned away from my quickly and told me, "I don't do that shit anymore. Nuh-uh. No sir. None of that shit for me. I just takes my methadone and have a blast on the pipe and ... no, *no sir*. No heroin for me. That shit *kills* you, man. And the fuckin' assholes around here ... fuckin' kids. Man, they'd sell you any old shit and tell you it was dope man, anything at all. That's what happened to my girl Natalie. Bought a bag from some fucking beat artist and shot it up and wham! You know what? You know what was in that fuckin' shit? Fuckin' *rat poison*, man. Rat poison! Her arm got all dried out and withered up and shit ... real ugly. Fuckin' cocksuckers. At least with rock the worst that can happen is you end up smoking a piece of wax or soap. But rat poison? I tell ya ... that little prick got his, though. Little spic motherfucker."

She went back to her drink. I waited a couple of beats and asked again.

"You know where I can score?"

"You see the motel across from the strip mall outside? The Starlight? There's a kid that sells out of there. He's a little asshole but he won't burn you. He's in Room 217, but he's got runners hanging outside of the motel."

"Okay."

"But *don't use the runners!* Those little fucks'll just take your money and split if they don't know you. Knock on room 217 and tell him you know Alicia. Now, you gonna buy me a drink?"

I got up to get her a drink and noticed her legs when I was standing up. They were bowed and covered—from ankle to crotch—in lumps, cigarette burns, track marks, and craters. She had a metal walking stick under the table and I had to wonder how many years Alicia had been doing this shit. I bought her a large vodka and Coca-Cola and brought it over to the table.

"Thanks, Alicia, I gotta split."

She grinned a wide yellow grin at me and raised her glass.

"Take care," she said as I left the bar.

The Starlight Motel was, if anything, more dissolute than the bar I just left. As Alicia had warned me, there was a gaggle of fourteen and fifteen-year-old kids in hooded sweat tops hanging out up front who noted my approach and fanned out almost in perfect synchronization to meet me. They where mostly skinny, white, and probably inbred.

"Yo, what you want man … you looking for somethin'?"

"Hey, hey … what you need?"

"Lookin' for rocks? Lookin' for rocks?"

I kept walking and muttered, "No. No I'm cool," and made it to the parking lot of the motel. The sounds of stereos blasting 80s metal and TVs blasting court shows crept out the darkened windows all around me. I walked up to the second level, found 217 and rapped on the door.

The door opened a fraction and a wired, nervous face peeked out of the crack.

"What you want, nigga?" it asked me.

"Alicia told me to come by. I'm lookin' for some stuff; she said you could help me out."

"Alicia?"

The door slammed shut and I heard a lock scraping open, and the door opened wider this time. The kid who stood in front of me was a wiry white boy in a Tupac Shakur T-shirt, wearing a red bandana over his shaved head.

"Alicia who?" he asked, jutting his chin up and sticking his chest out, "I know a lot of bitches. Alicia *who* nigga?"

"Old girl; hangs out at the bar across the road. Real fucked up legs."

The kid sucked in the air through his buck teeth in disgust.

"That nasty ol' crackhead ho? That bitch is always comin' on like *'D-Low I need credit man, gimme a rock man, I'll suck your balls for it, D-Low.'* Sheeit, skeevy fuckin' bitch. Now she's sending fuckin' crazy honkies from the bar over here. I gotta have a word with that bitch, yo."

I could see shitty and pissy diapers lying across the murky grey carpet in the room behind the kid. On the TV, "Cops" was playing with the volume turned low.

I cleared my throat. "So can you help me out? I need smack."

"No shit, huh nigga?" he replied simply, before slamming the door in my face.

I stood there slightly shocked for a moment. Through the door I heard footsteps, a door opening and the kid talking real low. From inside, a woman's voice started yelling at him and a baby started crying. The kid screamed at the girl and the door slammed again. Footsteps approached and he opened the door.

"You a cop?" he asked.

"No."

"Cause you know if you a cop you gotta tell me. That shit'll get thrown out of court, yo. That's entrapment an' shit."

"I ain't a cop. I'm a junky. Can you help me out?"

The kid thought about if for a second and asked "How much?"

"Four."

I handed him the eighty dollars and he ushered me in. He went into the back where the infant was screaming and I amused myself by watching a drunken hick get maced by the pigs on TV. Freebasing paraphernalia was strewn across a broken coffee table, and the smell of ammonia hung in the air, making my eyes smart.

The kid returned and handed me a battered packet of Camels. "What're you? French or Australian or somethin' fruity like that?"

"I'm English."

"Well," he told me, "next time you see that raggedy bitch you tell her not to be sending over anymore French, Australian, or English dope fiends to my fuckin' motel. And next time, deal with the kids downstairs. That's what they're there for, nigga."

"Sure thing," I told the kid, glancing inside the packet before slipping it into my jacket. "Pleasure doin' business with you."

I opened the door and the kid followed me out.

"Peace out nigga," he said before slamming the door behind me.

FUCKED-UP, NEVADA

I woke up in the van still wearing last night's clothes. I was tired, sweating, dope-sick, and sore. The desert sun blasted through the windows, scorching the back of my eyelids and rousing me from my half sleep. My mouth tasted like shit, and I could hear the other three assholes snoring in varying pitches around me. With the sudden start of disappointing reality, I realized where I was. I grabbed my overnight bag, stepped over Jules's prostrate body, and slid the door open.

I stepped out into the cold air, slammed the door shut and walked over to the house. The front door was open—of course, why lock it out here?—and I stepped into the gloom. I could see the band passed out in the main room, empty liquor bottles and ashtrays full of cigarette butts on the table. I tiptoed to the bathroom and the door creaked open. A mangy cat with a meow pitched somewhere between a Theremin and a crying baby padded out and started mewling and rubbing itself against my leg. I kicked the fucking thing away and slid in the bathroom to fix myself.

The heroin I bought last night was so-so at best, but I dumped a lot into my wake up shot and managed to find a decent vein in my ankle. The dope flooded my bloodstream and I could feel normality returning: my aching muscles relaxed, the ice unthawed around my bones, my jangling nerves subsided. I looked at my watch; it was 6:30 a.m. Another perfect fucking day had begun.

Over breakfast at IHOP, Sam explained the whole thing to me. I was to interview the band before and after the show. They would film the gig in between, and I could watch or do whatever I wanted. When the show was over, we would pack up and head out and hit LA by tomorrow afternoon.

Again, I could not believe I had gotten involved in something so meaningless and stupid. Why was I hanging out with these people? I mean, what the fuck did they know about anything? At one point over breakfast, Paulie leaned over to me when Sam was in the bathroom and whispered something I didn't catch.

"Huh?"

"I said you got any smoke?"

I looked at this idiot and raised my palms.

"Shit. Well if you come across any ... let me know. Just keep it on the down low. Sam, he don't approve of drugs when we're working, you know?"

"Oh, sure," I told him. "I'll bear that in mind."

Some hours later I was sitting on the can in a toilet cubicle within the casino, pushing a shot of heroin mixed with some crystal meth I had brought with me for emergencies into a large vein which curled around the side of my left forearm. The blood coagulated in the barrel, causing the needle to block with five mls. to go. I withdrew the needle and watched a thick trickle of blood run down my arm, drip-dripping off my wrist onto the floor impassively, as I started to sense the speed roaring around my blood, sending my heartbeat into the stratosphere. As was my ritual I pointed the needle at the gleaming white tiles around me and pushed the plunger hard with my thumb. Sometimes, if that shit was really blocked, the plunger would depress fully with a pop causing the blood and heroin inside to spray back around the inside of the barrel. If it wasn't too badly blocked, as happened this time, when the plunger popped, a thin spray of brown blood streamed from the needle and created a pretty pattern on any surface it hit. Beautiful. I felt like a dog marking its territory. I had gone into some of the nicer hotels in West Hollywood to use the bathrooms and leave my mark on their pristine walls. It gave me a curious satisfaction, and I would absently fantasize about leaving blood splats in the toilets of Buckingham Palace, The White House, or Trump Plaza. On a whim, I dipped my finger into the small stream of blood on my arm and drew a crude red frame around the spray pattern, which had started to run into

84

itself and drip down the wall. I dabbed some more of the blood on my finger and scrawled an illegible signature on the bottom. Perfect. I was the junky Jackson Pollock.

I washed up and slipped my injecting equipment into the pocket of my leather jacket. Then I left the relative quiet of the toilet.

Stepping out onto the casino floor was like stepping into some kind of awful redneck hell. The noise of the machines was deafening, but even more deafening were the screams and yells and laughs and har-har-hars of the bikers, crazies, gawkers, and lost tourists who swarmed around the slot machines and gaming tables and formed long, disorderly queues to get to the bar. The band was due to hit the stage in thirty minutes, and I was supposed to be there when they walked from the dressing room to the stage in the middle of the casino floor to do one of those stupid Q&A sessions on the way to the stage. I fought my way to the far wall, showed my laminate to the security guard, and was ushered into the backstage area. In the long corridor, I found Sam, Jules, and Paulie standing around with the camera and boom mike at the ready.

"The band's getting ready now," Sam informed me. "Did you find everything?"

"Yeah," I told him, feeling a little jittery from the speed. "So listen … what exactly do you want me to ask these guys? I mean … we haven't really discussed anything about this."

"Just wing it," Sam told me with a big stupid grin. "You'll be fine."

Jules muttered cryptically to himself, peering at me through the viewfinder, while Paulie stood picking his nose and looking as dumb and useless as ever. The crystal meth and heroin sent my brain whirring in all kinds of different directions. What should I ask them? I figured I'd have thirty seconds at the most to get a question and their reply in once the band started walking. I decided that I should concentrate on one person. The obvious person was the drag queen Mick Jagger … but what to ask? I needed something great, something funny. Something that would capture the inherent pathos of their sad lifestyle. A zinger ... something perfect, a perfect question. But what?

Suddenly, the doors to the dressing room swung open and Mick Jagger came strutting out with the band following behind him, making a brisk move for the door at the far end of the corridor. Everything erupted around me and Jules leapt into life tailing the band. A microphone was thrust into my hand, and I saw Sam mouthing, "Go, go, go!" and waving his hand frantically in my direction. I broke into a trot after the band and started yelling "Mick! Mick!"

Mick Jagger half-turned but kept walking, and in a moment of panic I blurted out:

"So do you do this because you couldn't make it as a real musician?"

Everything stopped for a moment, and the band almost walked straight into their singer as he broke his stride. I panicked and stuttered, "What I mean is ... is there any dignity in doing this for a living?"

Mick Jagger gave a contemptuous look and instead of answering, he slowly raised his middle finger and placed it in front of my face.

"Asshole," he said simply.

Then he repeated the gesture into the camera and at Sam who stood there looking like someone had slapped him in his dopey face and then, boom!, the band was gone. Jules and Paulie stood around, unsure of what to do until Sam barked "Follow them, you pricks! We'd still better film the fucking show!" The three scuttled out onto the casino, and Sam and I were left in the corridor.

"That was pretty good, right? I mean, you can use that, right?"

For the first time since the whole thing started Sam lost his annoying enthusiasm. He finally looked tired. I smiled; now the fucker knew how I felt.

"I guess," he said, before walking out to watch the rest of the show.

I made it out there for a few songs, more into watching the crowd than the band, who churned out lackluster versions of all the Stones' classics. The audience didn't mind though; they were drunk and up for a good time no matter what.

I went to the bar to get a drink because there was nothing else to do. Biker girls stood next to their fat, man-mountain boyfriends and flashed their tits in order to get the barkeep's attention. Tit flashing seemed to be de-rigueur around these parts. When a bartender finally came over, I ordered a vodka tonic at a hideously inflated price.

I noticed a burly figure in full Angels regalia standing next to me, watching my every move with an amused grin. I looked up and he grinned a mouthful of tobacco stained teeth at me. I smiled back and nodded.

"Yuh look a little lost," he slurred.

"Really?" I asked, unsure of what he meant.

"Yeah, you do. You know ... San Francisco's thataway," he growled pointing to the neon exit signs by the far wall, "you goddamn fag *motherfucker*."

I just smiled and nodded blankly at him. What else could I do? He laughed a deep crackly smoker's laugh, and I picked up my drink and made my way to the side of the stage. The band was grinding their way through a take on "Brown Sugar," and a couple of trashy drunken blonde girls were dancing up front, mouthing the words back at the band. Mick Jagger blew them a kiss and attempted to replicate the famous chicken walk. It went badly. Then, on the stroke of midnight, an Angel rode through the floor of the casino on a gleaming Harley with, yes, a topless girl riding on the back of the bike. It got the biggest cheer of the night, and when the band resumed playing "Sympathy for the Devil," the sense of anticlimax was palpable.

We rode back to LA that night in silence. The band didn't allow the scheduled post-show interview to take place and decided to stay on in Laughlin with their friends for a few days before making their own way back to LA. With no good reason to be in Nevada anymore, we started the drive back to LA that night.

I started to feel better and better as each mile closer to home rolled by. I nodded out on a nice strong hit of junk for most of the journey back, and surfaced as we pulled off of the freeway near the Hollywood Bowl, minutes from Iris Circle. Nobody had spoken much during the ride home, and when the van pulled up outside of my place Sam yelled, "We're here!" and I roused from my slumber.

"Okay guys," I said, "it was fun. We'll have to do it again sometime."

Jules and Paulie waved at me as I grabbed my bag and got out. I stuck my head in the passenger window and said to Sam, "Thanks for everything."

"No problem," he muttered, barely able to make eye contact. He was still pissed that I had upset the band.

"Good luck with the rest of the movie," I said, and the van pulled away.

I slid my key into the lock and smiled to myself. I swore that I would never set foot in Laughlin, Nevada for as long as I lived. Oh Christ, it felt good to be home.

Part Two
ALVARADO AND 6TH BLUES

Alvarado and 6th: smell of meat cooking on the grills at the corner taco stands, two for ninety-nine cents and the feel of the sun against your back, walking on to the tune of mariachi music blaring from popsicle stands. Guys waving an inverted 'L' hand signal to oncoming traffic yelling, "papers!" LAPD patrol cars rousting the street drunks, pouring bottles of Thunderbird into the gutter as an old bum yells "please god, no!" with tears in his eyes...

Alvarado and 6th feels like purgatory. I have done so much time waiting here on its street corners and in its shady doorways hoping to score, dunking pound cake into my coffee in donut stands waiting for my beeper to go off, sitting in McDonald's and Wendy's and Burger King waiting for the bathroom to become free so I could fix under fluorescent lights...

Alvarado and 6th was overrun with people. I walked past the bar where a Mexican in a cowboy hat pissed against the wall, too drunk to stand straight, propped up by the top of his head, which rested against the bricks against which he was pissing. An older man stood in the doorway next to a sign reading *"Cerveza—Futbol"* eyeing me with suspicion as I went past. The people around here weren't dummies. They knew the score, and they could tell what I was straight away: a *viscioso,* one of the junkies who haunted this intersection, waiting anxiously by pay phones, cursing out loud as the sun dragged across the sky, and scoring before scuttling away from the daylight.

I paged Carlos from the pay phone at the intersection, then I settled down on the bench at the bus stop and waited. It had been a while since I injected that first time with Genesis, and life had moved on fast. My friends' attitudes had changed towards me considerably. I was totally open with them about what I was doing and as a result I saw them less and less. "Dropping the H-bomb" Chris called it, and the aptness of the pun was pretty stark.

Joan at first upset me by cutting herself off from me totally. She was going through her own shit with B. Their intake of crystal meth had increased steadily, and she stopped going out altogether. I suppose B felt uncomfortable out at parties and clubs because no matter where he was he'd rather be in his room smoking crystal with Joan, talking endless hours of nonsense, though the sunset and sunrise, fucking and talking between hits on the pipe. She spent most of her time in bed sleeping when he was up in San Francisco, and stayed isolated away with him when he was in town. Later, when I was on one of my rare outings from my apartment, she upset me by acting weird around me in the 3 Clubs.

It was one of the last nights I saw everybody. Since returning from Laughlin, there had been nothing much to do so consequently I was shooting more and more dope every day. Money was getting tight and my habit was getting bigger. The thought of hanging out in a bar with my friends was not exactly appealing. When RP insisted I turn up, I did so out of a sense of loyalty. I didn't want them to get too pissed off at my flaky behaviour, I suppose.

Everybody was drunk except me. I was drinking Pepsi, as I had stopped liking the taste of alcohol almost totally at this point. I had fixed at home on my way out and again in the bathroom upon arriving at the bar. I started nodding out at the table, missing snatches of conversation, and beginning to regret leaving the house at all. Kat, RP, and Sal Mackenzie all ignored my behaviour as they where coked up and drunk. I thought I could handle myself. Joan, on the other hand, kept shooting me these looks, looks which I can only describe as pitying looks, even holding her hands out to me, fixing me in a big watery gaze and telling me that she was worried about me. I was, of course, mortified that this speed freak had the audacity to feel sorry for *me*, and I left the bar soon afterwards without saying goodbye, cursing her for the whole journey home. Self-righteous cunt.

I started losing contact with RP, Sal, Kat, and the others partly though their inability to understand my remaining so determinedly high on heroin all the time, and partly through my own choice. Heroin is a solitary drug: it reduces the need for human interaction. I existed in a blissful cocoon of negative pleasure. At first I remained in close contact with Chris, as he was the only person I knew who used every day. Soon though, I found myself getting irritated by his manic episodes when he was on it and his whining when he was sick. He didn't work, living instead off a small allowance from his father. Consequently, he had to find other ways to fund his habit. Hanging out with him began to cost me, as he expected me to keep him in heroin as long as we scored using his dealers.

He eventually relented and gave me a beeper number for one of his regular connections. The guy's name was Pedro; he was a young overweight Mexican kid who seemed somewhat reliable and sold good shit. Once I had his number, I began to hang out with Chris less and less. The last I saw of him for a while, he was driving an antique table from his house to sell for dope money. He looked pale and shaky and didn't talk for long. He pulled up outside my house on his way to the furniture shop and stopped long enough to ascertain that I didn't have any drugs for him and that I couldn't lend him twenty dollars.

Soon I stopped wanting to go to bars at all. The antics of my friends bothered and irritated me. We had stopped being interested in the same things some time ago. I looked upon their boundless appetites for booze and uppers as childish and tiresome. I began to prefer quiet nights in—just me, my music, and my drugs—over bar crawls and house parties. Soon, I had settled down into a solitary routine. I rose in the mid morning, fixed my first hit of the day, sat down to write for a couple of hours before fixing again, and then figuring out how to get more money to score with. Genesis was around less and less; mostly out at the hostess bar or whoring, or up three, four nights on end high on crystal, yak yak yakking.

And then, as suddenly as she had appeared in my life, she was gone. The last time I saw her was the night she OD'd.

It was late on a Friday night and she came in high and drunk, dressed in her work outfit, which consisted of a cheap black cocktail dress and high heels. She knocked on the bedroom door and woke me up, sitting on the end of the bed obviously looped on speed and bothering me. She asked for a shot of heroin and I agreed, really only to stop her talking.

I mixed up a weak hit, and she skin popped it, lifting up her dress and exposing her bare white ass, sliding the needle into her buttock and depressing the plunger, hissing in pain. I watched her impassively as she did it, her sexuality utterly obliterated for me now by the heroin in my blood. She was lolling on the bed, waiting for the heroin to take the edge off the speed as I prepared a shot of my own. She talked at me the whole time, while I concentrated on cooking and fixing my own drugs.

"This guy was so rich ... he took me and a couple of the other girls from the club up to this place on Lookout Mountain. I guess he must be in movies or something. It was pretty regular ... he had booze and really good coke and we just hung out and got high all night ... he dressed us all up in lingerie that he'd bought ... and then he had me eat Connie out and the he brought out some dildos and had Connie, Trina, and me fuck each other. I didn't even have to fuck him, just suck his cock a little. And I stole a bathrobe. It's beautiful, looks like Chinese silk ... fuck him anyway; he came in my hair so I gotta wash it now ..."

I put the needle in my arm and got a register. I fixed and lay back on the bed. It took me a while to realize that Genesis had stopped talking. I enjoyed the silence at first; just the rumble of traffic on the 101 interrupting my thoughts, and it started to sound like the roaring of some distant sea, so I didn't mind.

I suppose she may have gurgled a little when she went under, but I don't remember. I'm pretty sure she didn't convulse or gasp because I didn't rouse for a while. Actually, it was the silence that started to bring me around, because she never remained quiet for that long. When I finally sat up and looked at her, she was turning blue, her eyes completely unfocused and looking in two opposite directions, towards oblivion. When I say that she was turning blue, I mean that literally. Her lips where purple, her cheeks the same colour I remember my grandfather's being when they laid him out for his wake in Ireland, and flecks of drool and vomit crusted around her mouth.

I was in the bathroom trying to drag her nude body under the cold water pouring from the shower, screaming at her to wake up and stop fucking around, panicked by the reality that she may well not wake up, my yells reverberating off of the blood-splattered tiles. I prayed to God for her to live and started trying to figure out what I would do if she didn't.

She seemed to be breathing when I left, but I still couldn't get her to talk or focus her eyes on me for more than a few seconds at a time. I got the idea into my head that she might have suffered brain damage. I laid her on the bed and tried to shoot her with some crystal meth I found in her purse. Her pulse was too weak for me to get a register so I shot the mixture into her muscle instead, not knowing if it would have any effect. I took the rest of the speed and mainlined it. With the methamphetamine rush came an almost unbearable rush of paranoia and a kind of drug fucked certainty that I had scrambled the girl's brains. I looked at her on the bed, lying on her side, breathing shallow, looking like a mess, her skin beyond white, make-up running all over her face. She looked like a coroner's photograph, and with that thought I bailed, grabbing handfuls of old syringes and any of the drugs that were lying around and I got the fuck out of there.

I drove to a porno store called Stan's Adult World high on speed, Xanax, and heroin, watching a video of a seemingly endless gang bang, shoving dimes into the slot, wedging my foot against the booth door to deter any offers from the other guys for a five-dollar blowjob. I drove around the entire next day going from hardcore theatres, to Mexican dive bars, to scoring spots ... not sleeping, in a narcotic half-conscious state, drinking whiskey in The Gold Room, watching off-duty cops play pool at six in the morning at the Short Stop on Sunset, Willie Nelson on the jukebox, endless scenes of girls and guys fucking in relentless close up, twisted permutations of asshole and pussy and cock and balls on video screens and LA talk radio crackling out of my stereo, "Lord Jesus I can feel my power coming, my power coming ..." At some point I found myself parked by the gas station on Alvarado and 6th with a dealer called Raphael in the back seat talking tequila–cocaine nonsense, buying crack and heroin, and still later again I was parked on a dark street with my car's interior light on, trying to fix in the gloom.

When I returned to the apartment, the landlord had posted a notice to vacate the apartment in three days or be locked out by the LA county sheriff's department. It had been almost twenty-four hours since Genesis OD'd when I slid my key into the lock. The place was in disarray, but to an even higher degree than usual. I called for her, but there was no reply. Stepping over the trash into the bedroom, I was relieved to find her gone. At least she was alive. I was not as relieved to find her bag of clothes, my CD player, fifty dollars and a bunch of my better suits gone, also. The bitch had robbed me and left, without as much as a note. And I had three days to vacate the apartment.

SOUTHPAW

Throughout the chaos of the last few months, Southpaw had ceased to be a going concern. Members drifted away to other bands and the nucleus of Dito, James, and myself rarely got together. Dito stayed away from me, sensing my need to be alone, never passing judgment or asking what the fuck I was doing to myself. It was obvious that something was wrong, though. I didn't call anyone. I avoided meeting people unless I was scoring from them. In my heroin and cocaine daze, days stretched into weeks and weeks into months without any meaningful activity on my part. Despite the heat, I was careful not to wear short sleeves around the band, but I still caught myself nodding out during rehearsal and having to stay for fifteen, twenty minutes at a time in the bathroom while I cooked up and tried to find a vein. There were other factors in the band's slide into inactivity than my drug use—infighting, bad managers, the difficulty in getting anyone to believe in "our kind of music" in the midst of the rap-metal revolution—but the heroin certainly didn't help. One day the band simply stopped playing, and that was that.

Out of the blue, Dito called me one afternoon, excited and talking a mile a minute.

"Hey man, you gotta do this show with me at the Viper Room next Wednesday! It's a real big deal! A lotta people are gonna be there ... Are you up for it?"

Sensing I had no choice, I agreed. A rehearsal was hastily arranged for the weekend and I shot up a speedball before going over to the rehearsal space, turning up sweaty and manic, babbling a lunatic monologue about the cops and the absurdity of jaywalking laws, knocking things over and cursing, running to the bathroom to fix with shaking hands, making a mess of my arm and returning to the room with blood soaking through my shirt muttering, "Let's play, let's do this..."

Trying to play the keyboard, my fingers felt leaden and unresponsive. The instrument itself, newly rescued from the pawn shop just for this occasion, was alien and awkward to the touch. I remembered how easily playing came in the days of The Catsuits. It was a purely automatic response. One time in particular, doing a show for Radio One with some Welsh neo-psychedelic band as our support, I cockily fixed my hair while holding down my keyboard part one handed ...

I felt, here in this claustrophobic LA rehearsal room, old and burnt out. The cocaine made my nerve endings scream in raw, amped-out fury while my heart pounded my ribs in an attempt to escape my toxic, wasted and poisoned body. I was an impostor, a fraud, a sickening phoney. What had I done with the kid who played that show three years ago? I had pummelled him into submission with hard drugs and bad decisions. The pilot was dead. The plane was doomed.

The day of the show, disaster struck. I was out of money and needing to find someone willing to advance me enough heroin to get through the day. I had last fixed at nine a.m., and by five p.m. I was getting desperate. Junk sickness swept through me like a black wind. A migraine so severe that I could barely open my eyes pounded at the inside of my skull, and suddenly I began to vomit. I covered my mouth but hot puke cascaded through my fingers and splattered the floor, covering the newspaper I had been reading before the migraine hit. It was now six o'clock and I had three hours before we were due on stage, two and a half before the sound check. Dito had begged me not to be late, not to be fucked up, and I swore to him that it would be okay.

Where the fuck was Henry? Henry was a young Peruvian kid I sometimes bought from who had reluctantly agreed to drive out to me and deliver a balloon of heroin on credit. This was at noon and six hours later I was still waiting with my needle, spoon, lighter, and water sitting on the counter top awaiting his dope. I desperately beeped him again, adding '911-911' after my number. I tried to imagine the sound of his car pulling up outside, the

96

clump of his footsteps approaching the door and the pause before
... *knock! knock!* ... as if by visualizing it I could somehow make
it happen. I screamed in frustration and cursed him to hell. It
was too late to try and score anywhere else; I was too sick to
move. Time crawled on. Forty minutes to sound check and my
mind reeled. I couldn't play; there was no hope. I could barely
stand up. I had now been waiting for seven hours and fifty
minutes for him to drive the thirty-five minutes from his
neighbourhood to mine.

At eight o'clock, like Jesus, like sex, like love, he appeared at
my door. I staggered to open it and there he was picking his nose
as if nothing was going on.

"Come in." I moaned.

"You look ..." he trilled, "*muy malo*, homie."

He dropped the balloon in my hand and split. I called a cab
and started to unwrap the balloon with shaking hands. At the
centre of it lay a clump of white powder. I tasted it. Cocaine.
Motherfucker! The motherfucking Peruvian cunt had destroyed
me! Destroyed me! There was no hope now; cocaine was no use
for my sickness. I shot it anyway, puked again when the coke hit
my jangling system and then staggered out to my honking cab
wired, weak, and crazy with dope sickness.

With Sunset Strip traffic I arrived at ten minutes to nine. I
started to wonder why I had even agreed to do the show. When
the band had stopped playing together it came as something of a
relief. I found no pleasure in playing music anymore. I realized
that I stood little to no chance of even experiencing a similar
level of musical success to what I had found with Mark Brel or
The Catsuits. I knew in my heart that my moment had passed. I
had already peaked, but here in LA, with the perfect unchanging
weather and the perfect unchanging drugs I ingested, time had a
way of slipping past unnoticed.

In the almost three years I had been floating around LA, I
had done nothing to capitalise on my successes in England. Three
years passed in an instant, but I knew in the music industry my
achievements may as well have been a lifetime ago. No, the only

reason to continue playing music would be the good old clichéd ones: a passion for rock n' roll and an unwavering belief in The Dream. Truth was, I had neither anymore. With all of the energy I needed to spend keeping my drug habit up, I had not a drop left over for something as all consuming as music. I was here out of loyalty to Dito and, I suppose, the fear that without even a band to tie me to my old life, I would finally be cut loose and adrift in Los Angeles, a ghost whose lines of history and sense of identity had been cut off for non-payment.

I had blown the sound-check, and as the cab pulled up outside the club, I saw Dito pacing the sidewalk like an expectant father. I threw open the cab door and staggered onto the curb, vomiting one last time over myself and into the street in the same movement.

"I'm here, I'm here ..." I spluttered and Dito muttered, "Oh Christ, man" as we made our way in through the back exit.

The show dragged, and I played badly in my vomit stained T-shirt and leather jacket. Irrespective of that, I stole forty dollars from a tip tray and headed out to score almost as soon as I walked off stage.

Outside, I hailed a cab as Dito ran from the club to catch up with me.

"Hey!" he yelled, "Where you going? You okay?"

"Yeah, yeah ... just something I gotta do ..."

"Oh,"

We stood there, regarding each other for a while. I was at a loss for what to say and hated myself for it. I knew as well as he did what was happening here. The cab honked and I said, "I gotta split Dito," and he nodded. We left in opposite directions— me towards downtown to get fixed, and Dito back to the club. I watched the lights of the Viper Room fade into the distance as the cab pulled away and headed east.

I miss you, Dito.

THE ELECTRIC KOOL AID
SPEEDBALL TEST

After that, I pretty much gave up on music for a while. I left my apartment the night before I was due to be evicted carrying whatever I could fit into garbage bags. The place was destroyed: blood splatters on the tiles, garbage lying all over every surface, used needles in kitchen drawers, the medicine cabinet and underfoot.

I began a nomadic existence between motel rooms while I could still afford them. The people I knew from various bands tried to keep me in the loop with the latest trends, and up-to-date on who was getting signed, but I never turned up to the shows when I was on the guest list. No one wanted to come to whichever motel I was staying at because it usually involved running the gamut of crack dealers and alcoholics who loitered in the lobby before getting to my room and gingerly picking their way around the piles of discarded syringes to find me incapable of having a conversation which didn't revolve around where to score more heroin. I started to get the reputation of a gutter junky around the music scene in Hollywood, and nobody wanted to hang out with someone like that unless they were a junky themselves. And that, I suppose, is how I ended up in Electric Kool-Aid for a brief but eventful run.

Simon was a kid I met through Lori, my speed connection, and as we had a drug habit in common Simon and I started to hang out and play music together. In a typically incestuous LA twist, he was also the latest in a long line of drummers with Electric Kool-Aid who, after finding themselves to be the darlings of the Hollywood music scene, blew it in a maelstrom of hard drugs, fistfights, and lunatic decision-making. I became a regular at Simon's place in East Hollywood, which was becoming a kind of halfway house for drug casualties and other human wreckage from the East LA art scene. We sat up night after night shooting strong trucker speed and heroin and recording angular, stoned songs. Most were cut around four in the morning after a full twenty-four hours or more of constant, heavy drug use. Often, Simon's place looked like a waiting room for junkies, and most days there would be three or four wan, pained characters sitting around itching and shifting uncomfortably, waiting for someone to show up with smack. They looked like crows on a telephone wire, their eyes shooting to the door with a pleading look anytime someone new walked in. Most of them were in awe of Atom, Electric Kool-Aid's singer and songwriter, and they waited around on the off chance that he would show up and they could bask in his reflected glory for a while. I was more indifferent than that, my focus entirely on making sure the flow of drugs remained constant. The latest ripplings in the music scene were a ludicrous abstract thought.

One day Simon and I were waiting for some heroin to be delivered, when who rolled in with Lori (who was scoring for us) but Atom, dressed in white robes like some kind of fucking cult leader. Peeking out from under the hem of his robe were the pointed toes of a pair of snakeskin boots. He looked taller, more gaunt and sickly than he did in the press pictures I had seen. He surveyed the room and some of the other junkies practically jumped up to offer him a seat.

He knew me through my band's previous guitar player though, and came over to perch on the seat next to me. Lori handed me my balloon which I knew the thieving bitch had opened, removed a fraction of the tar heroin, and then resealed. I started to prepare my shot. The last time I had seen Atom I was not shooting dope, but if he was surprised when I pulled out my pencil case and removed a spoon, distilled water, filter, tourniquet and insulin syringe, he didn't show it.

"Got your own kit now, huh?" he said, with a smile that was half wince, and then, "You got a spare needle?"

I handed him one, and we began to prepare out shots in silence.

After shooting our way to glory we all settled down, except for Atom who suddenly became very animated. He was eager to tell me about the tour, the trouble they had scoring drugs, and how the record company representative in Japan had given them some grass in a cloak and dagger manner usually reserved for international espionage.

"You should come play with us," he said.

"You've got a keyboard player."

"Not anymore. I had to let him go."

"Why?"

"He was a cocksucker."

So that's how I found myself roped into the Electric Kool-Aid travelling circus for a while. It was hot in LA; it's always hot in LA, but when you're always a little dope sick and out of money and cooped up in a house on top of Lookout Mountain with a bunch of other junkies trying to learn a song, it seems hotter— oppressively so.

At the first rehearsal I showed up, as would become my ritual over the next few weeks, riding shotgun in Simon's rickety Volkswagen Bug. We snaked up the winding narrow path that led to Atom's house on top of Lookout Mountain. The road had no barriers to prevent the car from tumbling onto the busy stretch of freeway below, and if we met a car coming the other way, someone had to reverse all the way to the start of their journey or everyone would be at an impasse. Simon had filled me in on a few of the wilder stories about Atom: the gun fixation, the death threats to the Oscar Wildes (a band who started off as good friends of Atom's but who had become an object of seething resentment as their success and his drug intake grew), the obsession with the Masons, and his messiah complex which became fully fledged when he was high enough. Trundling up to this large, secluded house I began to thank God that at least we had a drug habit as a connection. There's no icebreaker in the world like shooting up with someone.

Atom answered the door dressed in his uniformed white,

looking more distracted than usual.

"Rehearsal's off," he told us, ushering us in, "unless you can loan me forty dollars and give me a ride."

Both of his guitars were in the pawn shop. He was forty dollars short on the tickets to retrieve them. He gave me a brief tour of the house, which included him showing me his sitars, plucking long sustained notes on them and nodding to himself contentedly in a dreamlike manner, and finally showing me his Masonic sword. It was an awesome thing, heavy and beautifully carved with coded designs.

"A lot of people would like to get their hands on this," he told me in whispered, reverential tones. "You don't mess with the Masons. I shouldn't even *have* this."

We got ourselves straight with a couple of balloons of coke and heroin I had on me, and then rode to the pawn shop on Sunset where the guitars were.

The place was typical as far as LA pawn shops go—the wooden statue of an Indian Chief outside the door; the cool, dark, musty interior. Believe me, when you have a habit you spend a lot of time in pawn shops. The old Armenian man behind the counter knew Atom and sarcastically addressed him as "the rock star," to which Atom scowled back, "Fuck you, old man." The old man came out from behind his chicken wire-fronted counter and shuffled onto the shop floor. Despite the hump in his back, he moved quickly for someone so twisted and bent. I flicked through the CDs and stumbled across a copy of The Catsuits' debut album for sale for the princely sum of seventy cents, right next to a soundtrack for *LA Law* which was, understandably, a dollar-fifty.

"I got some good stuff for you rock star ... new guns."

"Oh yeah, yeah, let me see ..."

Simon, who knew Atom a lot better than I did, got a look across his face that I would learn to recognize pretty well over the coming weeks—exasperation mixed with the knowledge that it was utterly futile to try and curb Atom's insanity.

We left an hour later with only one guitar, some ammo, and a replica civil war pistol so old it was considered an antique and didn't require a waiting period. Driving up Sunset again, Atom kept trying to freak Simon out by sticking the gun out of the car and pointing it at open-mouthed passers-by, screaming, *"I Will Kill All Of You Fuckers!"* We used the leftover money to score, and that was how our first rehearsal started.

I discovered that the original line-up of the band had all quit after Atom began using heroin heavily and started a number of high-profile, career-wrecking onstage fistfights. The line-up I would be involved with was cobbled together from musicians who either didn't know how crazy Atom was or didn't care. Still, the band lost a member by a rate of one person every couple of days. We had three weeks to prepare for a headlining show at the Troubadour, a pretty well known spot in LA. The starting line-up consisted of Atom, Simon, a strung-out guitarist named Aaron, Mike from Southpaw on bass, a Hollywood freak named Buddy on second guitar, and myself.

Aaron was the first to go—he got too high to play and fucked up his cues a couple of times. Atom berated him for over an hour, calling him a useless nancy boy junky who couldn't even play the guitar; a pathetic, clichéd Johnny Thunders wannabe. He even told him that he was rotten at being a junky, never mind a musician. That was the last we saw of Aaron. He was practically in tears when he left. Aaron's real problem was that he was in awe of Atom, and if you were in awe of or feared Atom in any way, he would use that to completely destroy you.

Mike went next. He and Buddy were the two non-junkies in the band, and even his impeccable patience and veneer of unflappability couldn't take these rehearsals. We would generally start an hour or so late while everybody shot up, wheedled drugs out of each other, or nodded out during long circular conversations about where this sitar line should go or on the relative merits of the The Zombies' *Odyssey and Oracle*. Then the music would start. It would be a funeral dirge if Simon had done heroin before playing, or a breakneck jittery pace if he had done crystal meth. Then, each song would be interrupted several times while Atom berated Simon, myself, Mike, or Buddy for playing a note behind or in front of the beat, for not grooving enough, or simply to interject another piece of information relating to a conversation we had all had three hours ago. The whole scene got too weird for Mike, so one day we were a four piece: vocals, two guitars, keyboards, and drums. It would be almost four years before I saw Mike again, in London, touring as the lighting guy for the latest group of ex-Kool-Aid musicians to be in a flavour-of-the-month band.

Buddy got the worst of it once Aaron and Mike split. He was not a junky, just a pot smoker with a stupid, stoned grin stuck to his face permanently. He absolutely idolized Atom. The most banal bit of information offered by Atom would receive a slow rapturous nod, as if Buddy was a nun receiving a proclamation from the pope himself. It was as if by being in this room with Atom, Buddy had realized all of his life's ambitions and would therefore tolerate every piece of verbal or physical abuse Atom could throw at him.

As the rehearsals wore on, Buddy became a constant target for harassment. Sometimes he would bring it on himself. I think he saw himself as a voice of reason among the chaos, and he mistakenly assumed that Atom would see and respect that. Once, he pulled me aside and told Simon and I to stop sharing our drugs with Atom.

"You see how crazy he gets when he shoots dope, man," Buddy told me. I told him that if he wanted to see crazy he should watch what would happen if I *didn't* share my shit with Atom.

His biggest mistake, and the moment that spelled the end for Buddy, was when we took a break so we could all go fix. I told Buddy to hang and read a magazine, as it had been known to take me half an hour or more to find a usable vein.

"Hey Atom," Buddy yelled, "don't you think you've had enough? Let those two jokers go get high ... I can show you a song I wrote I think you'll like."

Atom didn't dignify Buddy's moronic statement with a reply, but the look on his face said it all. The next day, Buddy was gone.

Now we had a real problem. The show was in three days and

we had to rearrange the entire set to be played on guitar, drums, and keyboards. We did more and more drugs. I started shooting coke, and I was finding it hard to sit still long enough to finish a song without sneaking off and fixing while no one was looking. Atom wanted to find a Hammond organ and have me play it "like the fucking *Doors*, man." At this point we had four songs, and they sounded ropy at best. I began to realize the show was going to be a disaster and broached the subject of pulling out. Atom stated that there was no way—we needed the money.

It all ended in a suitably farcical manner. We were rehearsing when Atom suddenly decided he wanted some fresh orange juice and that he wanted Simon and I to get it. I figured he had some drugs that we weren't meant to know about and he wanted to do them. We got into the rickety Volks and started down Lookout Mountain. At the bottom of the mountain, we took a right and headed to a Ralph's on the corner of Sunset. As soon as we were on the road though, the car started spluttering and shaking.

"Aw fuck," Simon said as the engine died and he rolled the car over to the curb, "I'm outta gas."

It was too far and too steep to walk back to Atom's place. After rustling up five dollars in change and an empty Gatorade bottle between the two of us, we took the twenty minute walk to the nearest gas station, filled up the bottle with two dollars of gas, and brought it back to the bug. We then drove down to the gas station put the other three dollars in the tank and returned to Atom's place. It had taken an hour, and when we walked in, we were hot, thirsty, and pissed off. My first thought was finishing the last of my smack and getting a glass of cold water. Atom was in his chair with his ceremonial sword across his lap.

"What kept you?" he asked.

Simon started the whole convoluted story of how the Bug died and we had to get gas and Atom nodded affably. When Simon was done, I could see he was quite agitated. His patience with Atom was dangerously thin, and Simon was just waiting for Atom to say something to piss him off.

"Well, where's the juice?" asked Atom.

And that was it.

"Did you listen to a word I just said, man??? We had to walk to the gas station and fill a fucking Gatorade bottle full of gas and walk back to the car!!! Asshole! *I did not get your fucking juice!*"

In the ensuing ruckus a Masonic sword got swung at Simon and I, and a guitar knocked against an amp so hard that we could still hear the feedback wailing out of the open front door with Atom cursing us, our mothers, and our unborn children as we drove away from the house.

Still, Simon and I showed up to the gig two nights later. Simon used to score from a girl who worked the door, so we slipped in without paying. As the lights went down and a few expectant whoops and hollers went up from the crowd, Simon leaned into me and said, "I can't wait to see how the motherfucker tries to pull this shit off."

Atom walked up to the mike and began to play the opening song with just an acoustic guitar, which from the first chord, went badly out of tune. In between songs, he berated the sound guy and the lighting guy, saying they were crucifying him. He forgot the words to the songs. I could sense the crowd getting uglier and more restless around us. "Where's the rest of the band?" someone yelled and Atom muttered, "I am the fucking band, asswipe," into the mike.

I was standing at the back with Simon, stoned and pretty amused about the whole situation. Then, out of nowhere somebody jumped up on stage from the audience and shambled over to Atom. I figured maybe somebody was gonna go punch his lights out, but then I recognized Buddy, with that same dumb grin stuck onto his face. He picked up an electric guitar during the intro to a song called "I'm In Hell" and started trying to plug into an amp. It was a beautiful, ridiculous moment. No one else knew who Buddy was, but the biggest cheer of the night came when Atom noticed him with a scowl and walked over, guitar aloft, and tried to smash it over Buddy's head. He missed and split the guitar open on Buddy's shoulder and with a yelp, Buddy staggered off of the stage.

I left before the show was over. After half an hour, the floor started emptying out and all but the politest smattering of applause had stopped when Atom abandoned his latest songs midway through. The sight I left with was of an object arcing its way towards Atom as he strummed a half-forgotten song. The object froze momentarily in the air before hitting his guitar and disintegrating in a shower of red. I thought it was a nice touch that someone had gone to all the trouble of bringing a tomato to the show for the sake of tradition.

Outside, it was a beautiful, clear night in Hollywood. We took the 101 east heading to Sunset and Benton to cop.

"You know, Simon," I said, as the city lights danced off the bug's windshield, "sometimes being in a band isn't all it's cracked up to be."

But Simon wasn't listening. He was yelling into his mobile in pidgin-Spanish *"Cinco minuto,* man! We'll be there in *cinco minuto!"*

NOTHING SHOCKING

Nothing surprised me anymore. I watched a guy mix up a shot of crystal meth and distilled water and, right there in the seat of this car we were parked in on Hollywood Boulevard, whip down his pants and shoot it up right into his groin. Broad daylight. I was spun off of shooting speed, too, but I had seen enough crazy scenes on crank that I was unflappable at this point. It was three o'clock in the afternoon during a baking Los Angeles heat wave. I asked him if it hurt fixing there.

"Only the first few times," he told me, "but I've done it so often now that the hole never really closes up. I get a hit the first time every time, so whatever. I just stick it in there and wham!Blood pops right up like I had willed it..."

I felt trapped and sick, my habit outstripping my income and my ability to work. Systematically, over a period of four months, I had managed to alienate every single person I knew who was prepared to pay me to write. All of my desperate calls to Propaganda Films trying to rustle up more video work were mysteriously rerouted to an answering machine without even an outgoing message on it. I was *persona non gratis* with them and nearly everyone else. I could no longer keep a fixed address, staying in short-let motels, friend's houses, even sleeping in the back of my car.

In an effort to straighten myself out, I briefly flirted with methadone treatment at a clinic in Hollywood. It was hardly an encouraging experience. The clinic was right around the corner from where I was staying at the time, a roach-ridden hooker motel on Wilcox between Hollywood and Sunset called the Mark Twain. I was there out of pure economics—it cost 174 dollars a week and they didn't require a security deposit. The Mark Twain was depressing with its many shades of brown upholstery in the

109

hallways, lime green rooms, dilapidated 1920s bathroom fixtures, and one barred window which looked out over a parking lot where on Sundays they gave soup to the drunks and the street kids who spat and grizzled and fought over it. Despite all that, there were some advantages that came with having this particular address. The only needle exchange in Hollywood was a five minute walk on Cahuenga, right across from a queer bar—which opened at six a.m.—where I sometimes hung out when I was shooting methadrine and couldn't sleep. Or, if I was tired and broke and trying to figure a way out of my predicament, there was the methadone clinic, which was five minutes or less in the opposite direction.

It was an ugly place, and the karma was wrong from the start. I was pretty fucked up by this time, shooting Mexican tar heroin and cocaine every day, sometimes up to fifteen or twenty shots a day, maybe more on occasions. Everything I owned was in and out of a pawn shop on Fairfax Avenue, including my keyboard and my word processor.

I made an appointment at the methadone clinic. At nine the next morning, I was to be assessed and dosed, so I stayed up the entire night in a state of fidgety excitement, fixing speedballs in the backs of my hand and my feet since my leg and arm veins where pretty much all gone by now. I figured I had chance to quit and sort my life out—the typical excitement of the junky who has just made a promise but hasn't had to follow through on it yet. At 8:30, I made my way down to the clinic, with two shots of cocaine in my jacket pocket. I had heard that the assessment could take a while. I had stopped shooting dope around three a.m., as they needed me to be sick before they could dose me. By 8:30, my pupils were as big as saucers and I was soaked in a sticky layer of junk sweat while the coke I was shooting worsened my sporadic twitches. I guess I looked like a crazy homeless guy and definitely a lot older than my twenty-two years.

The clinic was around the back of a check-cashing place that I knew pretty well on the corner of Hollywood and Cahuenga. I had passed a couple of bum checks there when I was desperate and ballsy enough, and didn't look too much like a junky and a thief. There were two black guys standing at the door, like I was trying to get into some trendy Hollywood nightclub. They looked me up and down before letting me through the open door and up the staircase. I wondered who they were there to keep out.

The clinic was a trip. It was a methadone clinic as well as a place for pre- and post-op sex changes to get medication and counselling. The waiting room was full of hard-looking Latino drag queens with permanent makeup and huge tits, and it was hard to tell who was post-op and who was pre-op. They all looked like they could kick the shit out of me. It was some scene, man. Outside, these same queens would hawk their medication to the junkies as they left, mostly sleepers or hypnotics. Occasionally a Dilaudid would turn up for sale, but they could fetch forty dollars a pill since they were so hard to get a hold of.

The methadone patients were a combination of the typical LA / Hollywood gutter junkies mixed with the rock and roll kids who developed a habit off smoking heroin on aluminium foil. I was assessed by some old Asian doctor who told me, after checking my injection sites and my level of sickness, that I should start off on eighty mls. First I would get forty, and then I had to wait. If I was still standing after thirty minutes I would get my other forty. I paid him twelve dollars, went up to the glass counter with my slip, and waited in line. In front of me, a woman who looked to be eighty years old, in pancake make-up and a black witchy bonnet, was handed a cup through the glass partition. She was supporting herself on a walking stick, and in her efforts to take the cup she had to place the stick against the counter and balance herself precariously against the wall. Her hand trembled as she reached for the meth and froze as she tottered on her heels in gravity-defying slow motion. It seemed she was about to slip. Instinctively, I moved forwards to support her, but I was grabbed by one of the workers and hauled back to where I was standing. The guy who grabbed me, an improbably large hick white kid with crossed eyes, pointed to a black line in the floor and mumbled "Don't cross the line. Cross the line again and ya don't git dosed."

Meanwhile, the old lady was still going through the long

pantomime of trying to raise the plastic cup of pink liquid to her lips while remaining upright. The trembling cup crawled towards her puckered lips. I felt my guts churn and loosen more, and got the idea that I might fall over soon, myself.

"C'mon you old fuck!" someone behind me yelled, getting a few "Yeahs!" of approval. I thought that was kind of fucked up, but when she finally got the methadone down and insisted on adding some water to her cup, swirling it around, and repeating the whole bullshit thing again, I found myself cursing her also.

They passed me my dose through the glass partition and I downed it quickly. It tasted strong, aniseed-like. My first hit of methadone. I was about to walk away when the Chinese lady behind the counter said, "Wait!"

I looked at her questioningly and she pointed at her mouth sternly. "Mouth." She wanted me to open my mouth to be sure I wasn't going to spit it out later and sell it for dope money.

Waiting for my juice to hit, I settled down into the bathroom to take a hit of coke. My only working vein was between my second and third finger on my right hand, and to get to it I had to slip off a gold and onyx ring I wore on that hand. I stared at the ring for a second. It had been passed on to me when I was just seven by a family friend I had loved dearly—Frank Barnet. He had lived next door to my godmother, Sarah, and had kept me entertained every Saturday when my mother was out shopping and my father was working. Frank had become another father figure to me, and when he died of cancer I was so distraught I couldn't go to school for three days, crying myself to sleep in a grief-stricken daze. He was the first person I knew who died on me. The concept that he just wasn't there anymore made no sense to me. That the ashes they spread on the ground were all that was left of my Frank, who laughed with me and bought me toys, made no sense at all, yet hurt with a painful intensity. I remember the day when they held the service, a misty churchyard, a handful of mourners and the confusion of knowing that people die suddenly and without reason.

His son had given the ring—the one he wore on his pinkie—to

me some weeks after the funeral. He said that one of Frank's last wishes was that I should have it. Of course it didn't fit, but I kept it next to my bed until I turned seventeen and filled out enough to slip it onto my own hand. Throughout all of the turmoil—the record deals, London, the tours, Los Angeles, addiction and divorce—I kept the ring on me at all times. I had never taken it to the pawn shop.

I still felt some of that youthful distress in my chest as I slipped it off my finger and placed it on the toilet cistern, cinching the belt around my arm. What would Frank think of this? Maybe the same kind of sadness that I felt when he died. Maybe the same lack of comprehension. I don't know.

I pumped and flexed to get the vein up and slipped the needle in, drawing blood after a few minutes spent poking around painfully in my knuckle. Black-red blood flooded into the barrel and I slowly pushed the coke home. I felt it hit, tasted it, and stared open-mouthed at the door. The door. Someone was pounding on the door.

"Hurry up in there! Number 23? Time for your dose!"

"Yeah..." I yelled, jumping up, slipping my belt though my jeans and grabbing my works before heading out.

I was back at the Mark Twain later when I realized that I had left the ring in the bathroom. The clinic was closed for the day, I was tired and broke, and this was the final straw. I tore the room apart in a hopeless rage, ending up lying on the bed in the foetal position, groaning with despair as I imagined where the ring could have ended up. Sold for a ten-dollar rock. Flushed down the toilet. On the hand of some fucking gutter junky bastard thief. Jesus fucking Christ! I was the stupidest person alive.

Of course, when I went back the next day the ring was gone. Of course no one had handed it in. In a moment of naivety I even put up a sign offering a reward that I couldn't afford for its return, stressing the lack of value in the ring and its sentimental meaning to me. No one ever called, and that part of my life was now gone forever.

Soon my days turned from the horror of scoring, hustling, and fixing to a different kind of horror: the waking death of the methadone clinic. Never quite sick, never quite high, I sleepwalked through the first two weeks before they started cutting me down ten mls. a week.

When I was down to forty mls. a day, I was sick all the time. One day, I got to the clinic five minutes late. I had been unable to leave the bathroom that morning for fear that I would vomit, shit my pants, or both as soon as I got out into the hallway. At the door to the clinic, the two black guys barred my way, telling me I was too late, that I'd have to come back tomorrow.

I freaked out, screaming, "What the fuck do you mean 'come back tomorrow?' Tomorrow's too fucking late!"

I sat in the parking lot, considering my fate. I had twelve dollars and I was sick. I had three hundred coming tomorrow from some writing I managed to do months back, but that was no help to me now. I watched a tall, heavyset blond girl go through the same routine with the guys at the door.

But this girl was having none of it, and she had a hell of a lot more energy than I had. Man, she called them all kind of names. "You dumb motherfucking niggers! I need to get fixed! Don't give me that fucking bullshit, man!" They laughed at the crazy junky whore. She walked away and slowed down as she approached me.

"You get locked out, too?" she asked, looking down on me, thankfully blocking out the early afternoon sun a little.

"Yeah. Those guys are fucking pricks."

"You got your twelve dollars?"

I nodded and stood up. She had a little dope on her, which we cooked up in her car, right there in the Thrifty parking lot, and shot. Then we went back to her boyfriend's place, explained what had happened, pooled our money with him, and went downtown to score. She told me her name was Suzie.

"Nice to meet you," I told her, shaking her track-marked hand.

That was the last time I'd go near a methadone clinic for another year and a half.

MIRACLE DOWNTOWN

I was hanging out with Suzie and her boyfriend Mike in their apartment off of Highland Avenue. He was chipping a little on heroin, while she was trying to clean up, doing yet another reduction cure at the Hollywood methadone clinic. I was still strung out and had turned up in the hope of getting a free meal. Suzie liked listening to my stories, and her boyfriend tolerated my presence although I could never quite figure out why. Mike was a big guy, from Boston originally, covered in tattoos. He wore a pork-pie hat at all times. He loved the Misfits and DOA and didn't seem like a natural born junky. I thought he would be the kind of person more inclined towards speed, booze, and bar fights. I'm sure Mike thought of me as a useless junky scumbag, and I must admit I was a little scared of him. It wasn't unusual for him to belt Suzie in the mouth if she answered him back too many times, and he always seemed to be brooding, about to erupt into another bout of screaming and punching. Being around them was exhausting, trying to second-guess when they would explode into violence and where to position myself accordingly. One on one, I could tolerate Mike a lot more—likewise Suzie—but being with them together always made me too uncomfortable to relax.

I had been there two hours and I was beginning to regret turning up at all. The night before, Mike and Suzie had a fight because she was using dope on top of her methadone, and now Mike didn't want anyone using in his house. Implied in all of this was that I was a bad influence on Suzie and it was my fault she was shooting up again. Of course, don't blame the clinics with their tightwad doses of methadone and their bull-headed insistence that you must fail a reduction cure three times before you're even eligible for a shot at maintenance ... blame me. Why not? All in all, I felt pretty uncomfortable in their apartment,

115

regretting my decision to leave my last shot of dope loaded in a syringe in my glove box instead of bringing it with me. At least then I could have gone to the bathroom and faked constipation for as long as it took me to find a vein and have a shot. I wasn't comfortable sitting there listening to their bickering and their lame attempts at conversation while trying not to react to the looks Suzie was shooting me; haunted desperate looks, because she wanted to fix too. Well, there was nothing I could do about that; it was her fucking boyfriend who had freaked out. I couldn't even acknowledge that she was looking at me every time his back was turned because he had an uncanny ability to pick up on whispered conversations, and I really didn't need to be stuck in the middle of a boy-girl fight right now.

I was trying to figure a way to leave. I didn't want to offend Mike so much that I couldn't mooch off him anymore. Suzie started talking to no one in particular.

"You know what I'd like to do..."

I knew what was coming. Mike stopped talking and fixed her with a glare.

"What? What would you like to do, Suzie?"

"Well, we could go see Blood. I mean, it's been two days ..."

Blood was Suzie's dealer. Mike stared at me, looking for a reaction. I kept a poker face, praying he'd go for it and we could all stop doing this ridiculous dance around the fact that we all just wanted to get high.

"And I suppose you'd need me to go downtown and get it, right?"

"I could go with you. If you want," I ventured, "I got some money."

"Alright, goddamn it," Mike conceded at last. "Where are the keys?"

We took the freeway downtown in silence. Mike was gunning the old Chevy, driving it as fast as it could lurch. I rarely came downtown to score; I didn't know the scene so much. Scoring off the street dealers downtown was something that I considered too risky to do regularly. The cops were all over that scene, and the likelihood of a bust was always higher that in Macarthur Park or Alvarado and 6th. Homeless people hung around the scoring spots selling new needles for two dollars or reconditioned needles for a dollar in the hopes of making enough money to buy a bottle of Mad Dog or Night Train. I counted three LAPD cruisers on the freeway before we turned off to downtown.

"Man, there's a lot of heat tonight," I commented.

"There's always a lot of heat around here. I fucking hate coming down here to pick up. Where do you usually score?"

"I got a couple of guys I can buy from around Macarthur Park."

"Is it that tar shit?"

"Yup."

"I can't stand that shit."

"It's strong."

"So is this, and I don't have to deal with a bunch of beaners to get it. Those fucking beaners would cut your throat for twenty dollars, man."

"What's Blood then? White?"

"Nah, he's a nigger man. He's okay, though."

I contemplated this. I had never gotten ripped off buying from Pedro, Carlos, Raphael, Henry, or Paco. I remembered the advice I've heard in the streets since the first day I got into this: never buy off of niggers; they're all con artists. Mexicans are honest, but niggers will rip off a white guy as soon as look at him. I hadn't been ripped off by anyone so far, and I had bought from blacks, Hispanics, and whites. Maybe I had been lucky.

We parked up in a dark street with a few pensive looking hookers and winos loitering around. Mike killed the engine and turned to me.

"I'll be two minutes," he said, getting out of the car. "Keep your head down, there are pigs doing sweeps of this street every three minutes." And with a slam he was gone with the sixty dollars we had pooled together.

I sank down into the passenger seat as a black and white crawled by, flashing a light into the parked vehicles. I saw a prostitute fade into the doorway of a bodega as the white light started to bathe the street like an interrogator's glare. I started to feel edgy, and I reached into the pocket of my trench coat for the shot I had grabbed from my car as we left he house. It was too dark to get a hit and I was too exposed, so I jammed the needle through my trouser leg and emptied the barrel into my burning thigh muscle. I pulled it out and rubbed the painful injection site as it began to weep blood. I put the cap back on the needle and stored it in my jacket. It was a nice strong shot, strong enough to feel even though I had to muscle it.

A set of headlights in the rear view mirror distracted me. I checked it out, and with a cold hit of fear realized it was yet another patrol car, this time pulling in behind me, about five parked cars back. The vulnerability of my situation started to dawn on me. No ID, in a car with expired plates that doesn't belong to me, parked in a notorious scoring spot with a used syringe in my possession. It was too late to dump it out of the window; that would only attract attention. I slid further down into my seat and watched what was going on in the side mirror. Two pigs got out of the car and huddled in conversation. Where the fuck was Mike? I didn't know what would be worse, if he showed up right now and walked into this with all of the smack he had picked up, or if he was too late and they found me cowering here with my rig in my hand. It was a lose-lose situation and I started to panic, imagining how long it would be before I was in cold turkey withdrawals on the floor of a holding cell if I got taken downtown.

The pigs started creeping towards me, toying with me, flashing their lights into the parked cars, sticking their faces against the glass of the drivers' side windows. I prayed that God would let them find some other poor bastard, shivering in a car and waiting to score. They were taking their fucking time, shining, staring, conversing, laughing, moving on.

118

They were three cars away now. This was it; I was popped for sure. I wedged the syringe down under the car seat in a pile of old Jack in the Box wrappers, hoping that they wouldn't want to rummage around in there while knowing full well that they would anyway. Two cars away. I could hear them talking.

Then the miracle happened. I heard a radio crackle into life, spewing out pig code words, obviously so serious that both cops froze before snarling, "Roger that," into the walkie-talkie and rushing back into their car. I watched their patrol car roar into life, sirens on as they pulled out, made a u-turn, and sped off. I didn't allow myself to believe it until they were out of sight, and as they disappeared my dope started to come on heavy and slow, taking me like a skilful dance partner as I crossed myself and thanked God for making the cops disappear.

Mike pulled open and slipped into the driver's seat. Without saying a word, he sparked the engine into life and pulled out. He spat out a handful of seven-dollar bags and handed them to me as we sped off into the night.

"Man, I almost got busted back there..." I babbled. "If you'd have shown up two minutes earlier, we'd have been popped for sure."

"No shit," Mike said, looking at me like I was some kind of idiot. "I know. I was watching you."

"What?"

He pointed at himself. "Who do you think got rid of the pigs?"

"You " I asked, barely believing, "But how?"

"I saw them pull up. I got on a pay phone and called 911, said that some people had been shot a few blocks away and there was a cop down and bleeding. That's the only way you can make every pig in the vicinity disappear, man ... shit, who'd you think did it? The patron saint of junkies?"

We both had a laugh over that as we turned onto the freeway and headed back to Hollywood. My rent was due on the motel in three days and didn't have the money to cover it, but right now I had been blessed, not by a saint, but by another junky. I had a pocket full of dope and for that, I was thankful.

COMMUNING WITH GOD

Oh fuck. Out of money, out of drugs, the owner of the motel pounding on my door telling me that I have until noon to get out. Oh you stupid bastard! Why do you do this to yourself?

My bed stank and the sheets clung to my body like someone poured a bucket of cold and clammy sweat over me in the night. I had been awake for a couple of hours—since the unrelenting sun started pouring in through the windows turning the room into a greenhouse once more—trying to put off this moment, trying to ignore the heavy feeling in the pit of my intestines. But now time was running out, so I sat up and unpeeled the sheets from my body and ran to the bathroom, doubled over, sitting on the toilet and shivering. I was sick, the sweat and liquefied shit was pouring out of my pores and my ass. The smell was making me gag, and I wondered if there is any fate worse than being a sick junky in a motel in East Hollywood on a hot, stinking, Los Angeles morning like this one.

From my seat, I raised my head and looked over to the word processor on the table. Although this had been my only lifeline as far as making money went in the past four months, right now it equalled nothing more than two days more in the Mark Twain and enough heroin to get me fixed so I could figure out my next move. I was too sick to haul it all the way down to Fairfax to pawn, so I started racking my brains, trying to figure out a way to score some dope and make it to the pawn shop and get a stay of execution.

I looked at the clock; it was quarter to nine in the morning. A time when people all over the world, except in Hollywood, were heading to straight jobs, completely divorced from my reality of shit, sweat, vomit, and heroin. I didn't know if I'd swap my place for theirs, but then again over the past months, I'd started to believe that I was a little crazy.

The only dealers I knew who operated this early in the morning were Raphael and Carlos. Raphael was a no-go; I'd completely burned him down as far as credit goes. I owed him a couple hundred bucks and he wasn't in the mood for extending any more favours to me. The last time I asked him, he said he wouldn't even sell to me until I paid off half of what I owed him. Carlos on the other hand, was a maybe. I owed him forty dollars, but I'd always tried to keep straight with him. There was a very good reason for this: he was part of the18th Street gang and I'd heard stories about what happens to debtors.

I threw some clothes on without combing my hair or shaving, put on my sunglasses and left the room. I had five dollars to my name and felt shitty. As I passed by the front desk, the old Indian guy who ran the place started to yell at me again but I yelled back, "I'll get your money, just gimme a couple of hours!" before I was out onto Wilcox in the baking heat. It was Thursday.

The Mark Twain was across the road from the post office on Wilcox and a bar called Bob's Frolic Room 2. Already, the smell of cigarettes and booze was leaking out onto the street. I turned right, headed past the parking lot and a sex shop, and turned right onto Hollywood Boulevard. There, I made it to the pay phone and called Carlos's pager, typing in my mobile number, which had been barred from making outgoing calls. Then I walked, heading up the Hollywood walk of fame, looking at all of the dumb names and cursing each of them: Buster Keaton, Eddie Murphy, Marilyn Monroe, yeah, fuck you too. At the corner of Cahuenga, I stopped in at Popeye's for a pink lemonade. A couple was arguing over what to order, and as I settled in behind them I caught the boyfriend telling his girl, "Woman, you need to fatten up that skinny ass, not lose more weight. Sheeit." Sitting around eating fried chicken were a few of the morose kids who hustled around the boulevard—mostly young boys who came in from Ohio or Utah to escape their families and now got by sucking cock for drug money, but also a few girls, most of whom looked younger than fifteen, with skin so white you could almost see the workings underneath and eyes so black they seemed all pupil.

The place felt like a waiting room for lost souls, the smell of desperation and youth on the skids mixed with the smell of chicken and barbecue sauce.

As I got my soda, the phone buzzed into life and it was Carlos's familiar voice on the other end asking me what's up.

"Hey man, it's me."

"Whatchoo need?"

I started off by highballing him.

"Listen man. I need twenty white, twenty black. But I need credit, just 'til this afternoon."

"Come on, man," Carlos warned me, "don't fuck around. You owe me money right?"

"Listen, man. I got money coming after one, but I need to get fixed so I can go get it. You know I'm always good for this. I only owe you forty bucks, man."

Carlos conceded with a long sigh of exasperation. Amazingly, he didn't force me down to just twenty dollars of heroin.

"Okay, twenty black, twenty white. Where you at?"

"I'm getting on the metro. I'll be there soon. At the usual place. I'll beep you 555 when I get there."

And with that, Carlos was gone. I walked out of Popeye's with my soda and a new spring in my step. Things were looking up.

I got on the metro at Hollywood and Western, enjoying the feel of the air conditioning against my skin. I cut onto the train without paying, knowing I was taking a risk because the LAPD came on these trains personally to check tickets, but I didn't care. I was already anticipating my first shot of the day, figuring out where I would do it, already tasting the dope flooding into my bloodstream. Nothing could touch me now. I was immortal.

I got off near Alvarado and 6th and paged Carlos before cutting across the back of the station to the maze of streets where I usually met his runner. Then I settled down and waited. Hip-hop and salsa music was booming out of the open windows of passing cars. Kids were playing in the streets with no shoes on as the sun crept further into the sky. Across the road was a donut shop where if you asked for "blue donuts," they would sell you Valium for a dollar a pill. I liked this neighbourhood, but I couldn't imagine living here.

I once went up to one of these apartments to score crack and was shocked by the amount of cockroaches the place had. They scuttled out from under the bed when you sat down, or climbed the walls and eyed you from a safe distance with no fear at all. The connection said, "All of these buildings ... many cockaroaches ... ees very bad, very dirty." He had a sister who lived there too who was mildly brain damaged from a car accident that had left an ugly indentation in her forehead. We all sat around for a bit smoking rocks, but as the crack pumped the adrenalin around my body, setting off neurotransmitters like some kind of frantic flashing pinball machine, the sight of her waiting for the pipe to come around impassively while a roach crawled up her arm was freaking me out. I had to leave.

Finally, the kid pulled up on a pedal bike. He was young, maybe thirteen or fourteen, skinny with a Lakers top on. I walked over to him and copped the two balloons, slipping them under my tongue.

"Carlos says call him at one," the kid told me, and I nodded as we both went off in opposite directions—him back to Carlos and more deliveries, and me to the local Burger King to shoot up.

There was a time when I hated McDonald's and Burger King, but in Los Angeles they made sense. In a town where everything was new and plastic, they seemed like monuments to the spirit of the city. After I got my habit, they came to hold another significance for me: the only places you could be guaranteed a clean bathroom with a door that locks for the price of a hamburger. I often wondered if they knew the service they where doing to junkies all over the world, or if straight people ever sat on the can and wondered how many people had sat there before them, probing for a vein and looking for answers, or at least relief from the pain. Once inside, I got a Coke and asked for the key to the bathroom. I locked myself in and threw my coat to the

124

floor, looking for my kit in my inside pocket.

I carried around an old pencil case containing a clean, one-cc Turemo disposable syringe, an alcohol swab, lighter, rubber tourniquet, spoon, and filter. I tied the tourniquet around my left arm before preparing the shot quickly and precisely. I ripped open the black balloon with my teeth and unwrapped the plastic, getting to the pungent, sticky nugget of heroin in the centre. It was a nice size. I could probably do to use half, but I was sick, so I decided to stick the whole lot in the spoon. Then I added a little water from the tap and held the lit lighter under the spoon. I was faint with dope sickness as I watched the water start to bubble and boil, and the black lump of smack start to dissolve, turning the water into a murky brown colour. I could smell the vinegar-like aroma rising from the spoon, and in my weakened state I thought I might gag. Instead, I turned the lighter off and carefully balanced the spoon on the sink. I took the white balloon and unwrapped it to get to the lump of pressed cocaine in the centre. I snapped off half of it and dropped it into the spoon. I pulled the plastic plunger out of my syringe and used it to crush up the coke and swirl it around in the spoon until it had mostly dissolved. I put the syringe back together and dropped the filter into the speedball. The white cigarette filter immediately turned brown and fat with the mixture. I stuck the needle into the filter and drew the solution up into the needle, running it under the cold tap to cool the solution before attempting to shoot it.

I looked for the spot between my thumb and forefinger where I had been shooting recently. The spot was angry, red, and swollen, so I slid the needle in gingerly. There was a bee sting when the needle broke flesh, and I probed around with the needle, pulling the dropper back, looking for a register. It took a while, but when the blood shot into the barrel I could have almost cried for joy.

In the Burger King bathroom, I communed with God. The coke hit first, the chemical smell hitting me almost from within, as if I breathed in after depressing the plunger and emptying the barrel into my vein, and breathed out the cocaine fumes. My brain started buzzing as the pleasure centres were activated

125

again and again and again. Zing! Zing! Zing! and I got the sensation of vertigo, as if I was being lifted from the toilet way, way up into the air, my stomach flipping over. The second wave hit me as the coke and the heroin propelled me back from my personal hell and into the real world once more.

I became acutely aware of my surroundings, but they could not bother me now. I started to pack my kit away, storing the heroin wrapper and the rest of the coke with my equipment, replacing the case in my jacket. I flushed the toilet, washed my face, and hit the streets again.

Back at the Mark Twain, I bounced into the lobby, raising my palm to the old Indian guy as he saw me and started to come around from the counter.

"I told you I'll have the money by one," I said.

"No, no, no," he retorted, "you listen to me. Two things. First, your mail."

He handed me two envelopes, one that looked suspiciously like a check.

"And secondly, you get your shit out my motel right now!"

I started to get a bad feeling. This wasn't just rent anger any more.His brown face was turning red, and he stared at me as if he could kill me right there and then.

"You'll get your money!" I replied weakly.

"Fuck the money!" he snapped back. "Your money ain't no good here, you fucking dope fiend shithead!"

I backed off from him, but he advanced on me, pulling out an old, barbed syringe.

"I sent my sister in to clean your room, and she stepped on this! It went through her foot! She's at the hospital getting blood tests for AIDS right now!"

"I don't … why did you send her in my room, man?" I yelled at him.

"Fucking druggie bastard!" the old guy yelled and threw a punch at me. It wasn't so hard, but it surprised me, and I fell backwards and cracked my head against the wall.

"You get your shit," he barked, "and you get out, or I call the cops.What do you want?"

"I'm going…"

I didn't punch him back. After all, I couldn't really blame him—if I had a sister and some junky's spike had gone through her foot, I'd be pretty pissed off, too.

My lip was bleeding a little as I made my way back to my room and tried to figure out my next move. I was homeless again, with only a word processor to my name, no heroin, about seven hours before I'd need another shot, and a bleeding lip.

Oh you stupid bastard why do you do this to yourself?

I sat down on the bed and took my jacket and shirt off. I concentrated on my breathing and the metallic taste of blood in my mouth. I tried to clear my thoughts. If you force yourself to make decisions in a panic situation, the brain can turn on you and start sending out erroneous information like a malfunctioning computer. Many people have been fucked over by taking decisions offered by an overwrought mind feeding them information destined to trip them up. It took me ten minutes to shut out the chatter in my head. My brain kept intruding, sending snippets from the past year crashing into the fore of my mind like uninvited guests at a party, drunk and throwing up on the carpet. I saw Genesis, pretty, blonde, naked, and OD'd in my bath after I shot her with some of my heroin, my screams reverberating around the bathroom as I smacked her in the face and sprayed cold water all over her yelling for her to wake up, wake up, you stupid bitch. I saw an abscess getting cut out of my arm, doped up and unfeeling, yet quietly revolted by the smell of the rotten blood as they stuck the scalpel into the weeping, swollen flesh.

Eventually I forced these images out of my head and let my mind rest. There really was only one option left, but it wasn't one that I felt I could do: clean up, before I ended up in jail or overdosed in a shabby motel room.

127

I opened my eyes and looked around my little room. The Mark Twain had been cheap and convenient. It was a shame I had to leave. The thought of having to clean up was still on my mind, but I knew I couldn't face methadone again, and without insurance or a regular income any other kind of treatment was out of my grasp, also. I knew from previous experience that trying to come off cold turkey was a fruitless exercise: over the past couple of months, I had sequestered myself in motels in Vegas and San Francisco in an effort to get away from my connections, but I always ended up high again before the third night. Doing it in Los Angeles was even worse—when dealers didn't hear from me for a few days they'd start calling me. When they heard I was trying to come off, they'd start offering me freebies to protect their own incomes. I suppose all I could do now was wait for something to come along. In the meantime, I'd pack up my shit and get down to the pawn shop.

I ripped open my mail, starting with the envelope that looked the most like a check. It was a piece I had submitted for a music magazine in New York being returned to me with a rejection slip. I remembered the piece; I was high as hell when I wrote it, awake for three consecutive days on a methadrine run. Probably not my best work.

The second envelope was from England. I opened it and read the letter. Then I reread it in disbelief. It was from my mother, who had finally gotten around to selling my old car. They got 1,000 pounds for it, which translated into just under 2,000 dollars. The check fluttered out of the envelope and landed at my feet.

I suppose that was a sign if ever I was looking for one. Now I had to decide for real whether to I was going to try detoxing.

I packed up and headed for my car before calling Carlos again to pick up what may have been my last bag of dope. I would be able to think more clearly once I had had a shot, I reasoned, and if I was going to clean up, there was no point in denying myself a bit of pleasure before my trip into rehab. I headed to the check cashing place on Hollywood and Cahuenga, noting that it was past one already.

It was another glorious day in Hollywood. Just up the road, there was a street paved with stars for Chrissake! Could life be any more perfect?

THE SWEET SMELL OF OBLIVION

By eight thirty I found myself parked down by Pico and Sixth with Raphael, loaded out of my mind behind the wheel of my car, while Raphael sat on the bonnet, drunk as a motherfucker, trying to work his new mobile phone and get hold of his coke connection. After cashing the check, I picked up some more smack off of Carlos and paid Raphael back what I owed him. I picked up two grams of coke from Raphael and shot it. I had gotten so lost in shooting coke that I hadn't even found another motel room yet. Instead, I had just been driving around, shooting up in the car, public restrooms, or wherever. Now I was trying to pick up more coke, but the only person around was Raphael, and after five p.m. he tended to be drunk to the point of incomprehension.

Today was no different. He wasn't holding but insisted I drive him around so he could buy more weight. He stunk of malt liquor and cheap tequila, and his English had deteriorated to the point of nonsense. The trip started off with him making me drive down east Sunset and buy him some drive thru McDonald's, then with him having me slow up to a bunch of hookers so he could yell at them and lean out of the back window, trying to grab at them. They cursed him out in Spanish, and one grabbed him and ripped his shirt a little. He made as if he was going to reach for his knife so I sped off, the motion throwing him back against the seat.

Now my coke was wearing off and I was starting to feel edgy. He told me to head down to Pico, where we drove around back streets slowly looking for the connection. I wasn't sure where we were anymore, or if there was any real chance of getting coke from Raphael when he was in this state, but the grim compulsion that awakened in me when I start to shoot coke had kept me driving him around for the past hour and a half, even as the situation seemed more and more hopeless.

I was parked in a gang-run neighbourhood with Raphael on my bonnet, wild hair sticking up and his shirt ripped open, watching him trying to focus on the numbers he was stabbing on his mobile, experiencing a growing sense of hopelessness at the whole situation.

I sat there, clutching the wheel hard, debating whether to give up on this and find a place to stay for the night. "A few more minutes," my head demanded of me. "He might get through to his connection any moment." I imagined getting another shot of coke into me, then I shut up and waited.

An LAPD patrol car rumbled past us but Raphael was completely oblivious, jabbering at his phone like a madman, talking craziness, and looking like an escaped lunatic with his shirt hanging open and one of his shoes hanging off. I groaned, thinking that they must have seen me. I had two balloons of heroin on me still, and my shooting equipment was in the glove box. Not only that; I had been shooting coke all day, so my track marks were particularly bloody and noticeable. I watched the car turn left at the bottom of the street and became utterly convinced they were going to circle the block and come around for a closer look. I stuck my head out of the window.

"Hey Raphael!" I hissed. "Forget it! There're cops around here! Let's go!"

He looked at me, barely able to focus, and started to argue with me in Spanish. He slid off the bonnet and came around to the drivers' side window, breathing his beer and tequila breath right at me.

"Leesten man... he come! He say right now he come in two minutes!"

This was the third time in the past hour that Raphael had given me the same promise. I made a decision, stuck the car into drive and pulled out, leaving Raphael flailing around on the sidewalk. I sped down the road, took a left at the end of the block, and sure enough, as I turned, I saw the cops turn onto the street I was just leaving, flashing their red lights.

"Fucking alcoholic motherfucker!" I fumed, taking the next left and heading west towards Hollywood, "I hope you get popped, you fucking drunken prick!"

It's as I've always said, drunks got no class to them. They're worse than crack heads, stumbling around breathing their fumes on you. A fucking liability. I remember when I was living up on Iris Circle in the Hollywood Hills and my only connection was Pedro, the young podgy kid who drove a red Toyota Corolla. He was pretty good with credit, but towards the end his drinking started to get out of control. Because of that, I hardly saw him anymore. The worst time was when my car was broken down, I was completely out of dope, and sick. Man, I was puking and shitting myself, doubled over with stomach cramps so bad it felt like my intestines were coiling and uncoiling like a pack of snakes underneath my skin. I took my last seven Vicodin but it didn't even touch the withdrawals. I had called Pedro at eight in the morning and he told me he'd be an hour. At nine I called him, and he told me twenty minutes. At ten he told me two minutes. At eleven he told me he was at the bottom of my hill and he'd be there in a second. Every time we spoke, I could hear music and people talking and glasses clinking but I kidded myself that it was just his car stereo. He turned up after eight at night, eleven hours late, drunk as a motherfucker and hardly able to stand. I wanted to beat the shit out of him but I was too weak, and anyway, he was my only connection, so I was polite and thanked him after he took my money and handed me the drugs. The next day, when I got my car fixed, I went out and found myself another connection, swearing never to have another drunk as a dealer.

Unfortunately, it seems that nearly every heroin dealer in Los Angeles is a borderline alcoholic, so it's just a matter of rotating them and trying to catch people on good days. I cursed Raphael again and swore that if I ever have children, I'd rather they did heroin than drank alcohol.

On Sunset near Western, I found a motel called the Motor

Home Lodge and I paid thirty-five dollars for the night. I grabbed my bags from the back seat and smiled when I noticed two black balloons that Raphael must have dropped out of his pocket during his drunken lurching about. I picked them up and rolled them between my fingers. They looked like forty dollar balloons. Well, it seemed the night wasn't a waste after all! I was starting to feel real edgy; coming down from the coke and counting back it must have been at least five hours since I had fixed some heroin. I sprinted up to my room, let myself in, and threw my bag on the bed.

The room was dark, with a creaky, old double bed and a fuzzy, unfocused TV playing hardcore porn. It had the dirty, furtive feel of a place where junkies come to shoot up, guys take ten dollar crack whores, and washed up screenwriters come to drink themselves to death. I got my kit out and headed to the bathroom with Raphael's dope. Even when I have a room to myself, I like to shoot up in the bathroom. I suppose its just habit, but a hit isn't a hit to me unless I do it in a bathroom. Automatically, I had the spoon out, water in the spoon, ripping open a balloon with my teeth...

I was cold when I woke up. The smell of vomit flooded my nostrils and I blinked my eyes into focus. My face was on the tiled floor of the bathroom, and I was lying on my left side, curled into the foetal position. I coughed, spitting out some more puke and tried to lift my head out of the mess. I got onto my knees and noticed the needle still hanging out of my left arm, dried blood clogging around the stem. I pulled it out and threw it across the room.

The last thing I remember was cooking up a pretty big shot, but it was nothing more than I'd done in the past. I'd surprised myself by finding a vein in my left arm—I'd thought they'd all collapsed—and I'd pushed the hit in. Almost immediately, though, I knew something was wrong. That breathless feeling in my chest I get from a good hit continued to grow until there was a void expanding outwards stretching further and further, choking my every attempt to draw breath. I felt the warmth

134

envelop me, and tried to stand as my vision started to blur.

Somehow I'd managed to fall on my side, face down on the floor. It kept my airways clear enough that I didn't choke on my own vomit. I had OD'd, but somehow I had woken up instead of slipping away.

I staggered to my feet and checked my reflection in the mirror. My lips were thin and purple, my skin was white with vomit splashed around my mouth and up the side of my face and in my hair. I looked like death. Smelled like it too.

"You gotta clean up," I told the apparition in the mirror, "you stupid fuck."

I stayed up all night, scared to fall asleep. I'd heard stories of people who, after OD'ing and being brought out of it, had gone to bed, only to die in their sleep of respiratory failure. They'd simply stop breathing. I found a little bit of crystal meth and tried to shoot it but had trouble hitting a vein because my blood pressure was so low. In the end I had to shoot into my neck, although I really hate the sensation of injecting there and try not to do it too often. The rush was disappointing and short lived, but the speed took away my all-encompassing desire to lie down, at least. I alternated between watching people fuck on TV and listlessly tapping at my word processor. The sun rose and time dragged. As soon as eight o'clock came by I got my shit together and prepared a final shot of heroin. It was weak, and instead of mainlining it I shot it into my muscle. Then I headed out, drove to Pasadena to a detox facility I had heard about from a girl I used to get high with. I was going to get clean.

NEAR MISSES (Part Two)

I was in the emergency room of Cedar Sinai on Hollywood Boulevard with Suzie who had collapsed, shaking and gurgling, convulsing like an epileptic and choking after shooting coke with me all night. Suzie turned up every now and then, usually when she and Mike had had an argument over drugs. She would teach him a lesson by staying out all night with me getting high, more often than not having taken every drug and all of the cash in their apartment. These little interludes would last as long as the drugs did. Many times I had woken up, groggy and still high on smack to find that she had taken her stuff and cleared out, almost as if she had never been there at all.

It was a junky girl named Hannah who had first showed me how to shoot cocaine, and in a way it was one of the worst things that anybody ever did for me. I did coke for the first time when I was sixteen years old and it was a drug that I had used in increasing amounts after moving to Los Angeles. In LA, coke was cheap, and the quality was good. Although it may seem naïve, it had never occurred to me that I could inject it. The first time I ever did it, I threw up violently, having misjudged the amount. Still, despite the inauspicious beginnings, I soon learned to love the feeling of shooting coke intravenously, almost as much as I loved shooting heroin.

Injecting coke is very different from snorting it. It's the difference between a kick in the ass and a shotgun blast in the face. Shooting coke is a rush of pure pleasure in the brain, unlike heroin, which is a more physical and emotional sensation. The high from shooting coke is that it creates a state of pure need, which, while it lasts, means that you will do anything to get more of the drug and delay the crash. When I am on a coke run, make no mistake that I will steal from friends, lie, and do anything within my power to get more coke. It is not a matter of making a decision to fuck people over; it is simply a question of reacting to an overwhelming state of need. A sense of right and wrong is a laughable luxury when I'm out of coke and terrified to return to my natural state.

Suzie had shown up with a black eye, an eight-ball, and a pack of fresh needles, cursing Mike as an asshole and a spoiled child. We didn't get into what had happened too much after that, instead mixing up coke and tap water in a spoon, filtering and preparing our injections. Before that first shot, I had the usual twinge of reservation about starting this again. I knew that after my first hit, I would be totally at the mercy of the drug. I had no doubt that the final result would be misery, black depression, and bleeding arms and sores from repeated injections. On a coke run I injected every fifteen minutes for as long as the drugs lasted, and I had managed to fuck up most of the veins in my arms, hands, and legs doing it. Still, the anticipation of that first rush once I pushed the coke in, the taste in the back of my throat, the rush of endorphins and adrenaline, the ringing in my ears ... well, that brushed all other cares aside.

However, just past midnight, following a huge shot of coke, Suzie collapsed backwards before she even had a chance to get the rig out of her arm. Her eyes were rolling back into her head and she was making a death rattle gurgle, flopping about the floor, twisting and bashing her head against the wall. I was in a blind panic, pulling the syringe out of her, yelling at her, asking her what the fuck was wrong, dialling for an ambulance, her nearly biting completely through the flesh on one of my fingers as I tried to stop her from choking on her own tongue.

Our surreal ambulance ride down to the hospital had Suzie in the back and me along for the ride up front with the driver, wired on coke and coming down already, worrying about the implications if she dies, wondering if she's still flopping around under the restraints. The ambulance driver, a sandy-haired, leather-faced old guy was rambling, some monologue about how he used to play music with some group called the Almond Brothers, spinning off into some story about playing a show with

138

a band called America, and I was thinking, "Oh Jesus, how did this happen? Half an hour ago I was in my apartment with a nice fat hit of cocaine in my rig, and now I'm in a fucking ambulance listening to this old bastard go on about shitty soft rock."

In the waiting area, a Latino girl dressed like a hooker hung around while I waited to get news of Suzie from the stoic black nurses. The girl was talking to her father on the pay phone, telling him that she had to leave town because some kid she knew called Rico had just been shot five times and she figured she might be next. I watched her on the pay phone, twisting the cable around her fingers. She didn't look so good, either—another one who'd obviously been up all night getting high, then dragged from that world by unforeseen circumstances into this one of antiseptic smells, blood, and screaming victims. On her arm was a tattoo of a low rider with the legend "213 – VIDA" underneath.

A Village People-looking cop with aviator shades and a handlebar moustache walked in and shot a long look around the ER before walking up to the desk and speaking in hushed tones to the woman at reception. She nodded over towards me like death, and I got to my feet to try and made my way towards the exit as casually as possible.

"Sir, please remain where you are," the cop said, approaching me and using the opportunity of my hesitation to get a firm grip on my arm.

I noticed that we had become the focus of attention. The girl on the phone covered the mouthpiece and watched us with interest, and the assorted drunks and crazies in the waiting room eyed me eagerly.

"Sir," the cop said in a flat Californian tone, "could you roll up your sleeve for me?"

I looked at him, pretending not to understand, and the cop started grabbing at the cuff of my shirt to drag it up and expose my bloody bruised arm. I relented and rolled it up myself, presenting the white, fucked up thing to his mirrored gaze.

"How long you been shooting dope, kid?"

I smiled at his bullshit Dragnet pig lingo and I could tell he didn't like that, because he tugged my sleeve back down with a grimace as if disgusted by the look of my flesh and started getting aggressive with me, demanding my name and ID ... all kinds of bullshit. Of course I didn't have anything on me, and the cop didn't like that even more. Going through all of the possible permutations of how this situation could play out, I was gripped by a choking fear, considering and calculating in an instant how I would deal with jail or deportation. I remembered something Genesis said to me: "Always call cops 'sir' and don't get aggressive. Ride it out and don't give them even more reason to bust you." I decided to cooperate.

"Six months, sir"

"Six months, *shit!*" the cop snarled, "Looks more like six years. You're a fuckin' mess."

"I'm trying to get clean, sir."

"Yeah right. That's why your girlfriend is in there overdosed, is it?"

"I'm on a waiting list for a methadone programme. I'm trying."

"You're trying, huh? Come out here with me."

He took me by the arm and marched me out of the waiting room into the murk beyond. Was this it? Was I going to get busted? I was pretty sure I didn't have anything incriminating on me, apart from my track marks. Can they bust people for track marks? He pushed me up against the wall, knocking the breath out of me. He was snarling in my face, exposing large, flat, white teeth and breathing coffee and cigarettes into my face. I watched my shocked, squirming reflection in his aviator glasses.

"I'm sick of busting you fucking bastards. Sick of you dumb, thieving street junkies!" he hissed at me. In the distance I could see his patrol car flashing blue, white, red, and back again before he slammed his fist into my guts while keeping me upright with his left forearm pinned across my throat. Pain exploded up my belly and chest like fireworks in my skull, and the blow was followed by another and another in quick succession. I was

140

finally allowed to drop to my knees, gasping for breath, tears streaming down my cheeks, vision blurring, greying out. Focusing on the cop's boots, up his black trousers to his gun belt, a gloved hand resting on the butt of his handgun, waiting for me, daring me to fight back, curse, or even attempt to stand.

"Now get the fuck away from here," he hissed, striding back into the ER. It took me a while to make it to my feet and stagger off towards Sunset Boulevard. Later, I heard from Suzie that he came to her bed and ordered the doctors out of the room, demanding to know who she got the drugs from, lifting up her dress to expose her track-marked inner thighs, leering at them, asking her how much she made as a drug whore, how much she charged to suck cock. He didn't bust her either, but simply strutted out after staring at her in disgust.

It was time for me to leave. After he returned to the ER I stepped out into the warm night, without drugs or the money to get home. As long as Suzie was okay, I was pretty sure I could count on her to keep her mouth shut. Except now I had the extra worry that the cops could show up, having been alerted by the ambulance guys about the drugs in my place. More claustrophobic than ever, more broke than ever, I started the long walk back home.

It took me a long while to make it home as I could barely walk. It was seven days before I stopped pissing blood; two weeks before my kidneys stopped hurting.

DETOX

"What drugs do you do on a regular basis?"

"Heroin, cocaine, crystal meth, crack."

"Alcohol?"

"I don't drink anymore."

The woman doing my initial assessment looked up at me and raised an eyebrow. She was white, in her late forties, with bright red hair and a hard look about her. She looked like every hard-faced woman I have ever encountered in an institution. They all have a similar look about them, their faces, mannerisms and voices were all interchangeable.

"Drinking's bad for you," I added, for her benefit.

She sighed, looked back at the sheet she was filling in, and ticked a box.

"And you inject, is that right?"

"Yes."

"Where do you inject?"

"Arms, legs, hands, feet, neck sometimes ... anywhere I can, really. I hit a vein in my stomach once but it blew out."

"Groin?"

"Nope."

"And what do you want from treatment?"

"I want to get straightened out. I'm tired; I almost died last night I'm living in motel rooms, sleeping in my car. I haven't seen anyone for the past six months apart from other junkies and my dealers."

"Have you ever attended Narcotics Anonymous meetings?"

"Yes, in the past. I didn't like them.They didn't do anything for me."

This was true. I found that twelve-step meetings alternated between boring and scary. People tend to divide into three camps at the meetings. First were the people who really didn't have a drug problem, for whom meetings were social gatherings that allowed them to talk about their problems at length to a captive audience. They either had decades of clean time after a few months of real drug use and therefore no reason to be at a meeting anymore, or they never had a problem in the first place. They were social users, or they used non-addictive drugs like pot , or they just joined NA for other reasons. In Los Angeles, NA meetings were becoming the new cool place for Hollywood types to network. I remember being told that if I ever wanted to sell a screenplay in Hollywood, to get to the Tuesday night meeting on Western and Beverly. And it was true; the room was full of these fucking assholes slurping coffee and chain smoking cigarettes, thanking God that they were no longer a socially unacceptable kind of addict.

The second group were the assholes that only came to meetings to boast about how fucked up they were, and to get a bit of notoriety that they were too dull to achieve in the real world. These people really pissed me off. They shared wild, improbable adventures of getting loaded, running around with guns, getting shot, OD'ing, and blowing thousands of dollars on drugs. They stood up to talk, posturing and strutting, with a line of bullshit a mile wide, and they were always inexplicably popular in meetings. People thought that they were "characters." Of course, I felt that the real characters were the ones still out doing it.

The third group were the true believers, religious fanatics who had swapped drugs for God and who banged on about the program, spoke only in program speak, and hammered their vision of the program into anyone who would listen. Annoying, self-important cocksuckers all of them, switching an addiction to drugs for an addiction to the twelve steps.

"Well, we are a twelve-step based rehab, and the meetings are mandatory. When you go over to the rehabilitation part of the unit, you will be attending two meetings a day ..."

"I don't want to go over to the rehabilitation part. I just want to detox, and have done with it."

The woman looked at me and sighed again.

"We don't recommend that people attend our detox wing and then just walk out of here. It just sets people up to fail."

I was starting to get sick and restless as I sat in this airless little room answering questions and having boxes ticked for me. Knowing full well that twenty-eight days in the rehab wing cost over three and a half thousand dollars, I decided to draw a line under the idea of my going into rehab once and for all.

"Listen, I'm not saying that I don't want to spend some time in rehab in principle. I'm not saying that at all, but I can't afford it. This money is the last money I have coming in for a while and it's all I've got. I can't afford rehab. All I can afford is a detox."

"And you said you are a musician?"

"And I write, yes. So no, no real job."

With that, the interview was over. I paid my money, had my belongings tagged and put into storage—apart from a few changes of clothes—and I was walked over to the detoxification wing.

The wing was bright and clean, quite antiseptic in appearance. Behind a large reception desk was a guy who looked like a skater, filling in some forms. The woman introduced me and he told me that his name was Jay. We shook hands and she disappeared off.

"So how you feeling, killer?" he asked with a forced joviality as I sat down. Great, stuck with a bunch of happy-clappy California ex-addicts who will insist on calling me 'killer' or 'sport' or some other shit like that. This was going to be rough.

"I'm feeling like shit, Jay, how are you?"

I was trying to break the ice, but he eyed me like I had just told him I wanted to have sex with his mother. Pretty uptight for a guy with Black Flag tattoos up and down his forearms. He looked through the case notes that the old woman from reception had given to him.

"Hey," I asked him after a few minutes of watching him read, silently moving his lips. "What's the deal with the woman who brought me in here?"

"Linda?" he laughed. "Man, she used to be one of the biggest smack dealers in all of California. A pretty popular hooker, too. People still get nostalgic for the days when she was in business. Ask her, she'll tell you herself. She ain't shy. She cleaned up here seven years ago and hasn't left since. She's second in charge here, besides Dee Dee."

"What's Dee Dee like, then?"

"You'll see."

The silence resumed as Jay continued to read. He was a slow reader, and I started to squirm in my seat. I was sick, and being sick under strip lighting in a hard plastic chair didn't make it any nicer.

"So I get medication, right?" I asked, forcing Jay away from my notes again.

"After we take your blood pressure."

After an eternity of waiting, he finished reading and took my blood pressure. Then I was weighed—I was down to 130 pounds. Finally, he disappeared to the medicine locker, returning with a plastic cup full of pills which I swallowed with water before he could finish telling me what they were. Nothing exciting, I supposed. I had already asked him if they would give me opiates and he just laughed. I would be detoxing without any substitute drugs to ease the pain.

The routine was pretty humane. I was dosed three times a day with a cocktail of benzodiazepams, barbiturates, anti-nausea pills, and a blood pressure medication called clonidine said to help with withdrawals. At night I was given a dose of choral hydrate, which tended to knock me unconscious for three to four hours before I was awake again waiting for the dawn and more medication.

The first few days were nothing more than a blur of images

and half dreams. I met people and forgot them in the time it took them to move out of my frame of vision. The staff took on the sinister look of demons, and I wandered dazed and in pain from room to room. After the first night in which I had a four bed room to myself, two new people arrived. One was an improbably healthy looking kid with red hair who seemed too clean cut and all American to me with his wide, white grin and military-cut red hair. He told me his name was Todd and that he was here to get off booze and heroin. I didn't pin him for a junky; he smiled too much, especially this being his first day in a rehab. I looked at his arms with heavy lidded eyes. No track marks in sight. Smoker. A health freak in the making too, no doubt. I figured he would fit in with the twelve-step regimen pretty easily.

The next guy was older, a tall and skinny man from Boston who talked incessantly and sweated profusely. He was quite obviously from Irish stock like me, with his pale brown eyes, black hair, and pasty complexion. You could spot it even before he slipped from Boston to Irish brogue and back again.

"Billy," he said, taking my hand.

"How's it going?" I replied, heavily sedated.

Upon hearing my accent he pulled back his hand bowed his head in mock deference, then in a Dick Van Dyke English accent said, "I am most pleased to be invited to share your humble abode."

"Let me guess. You're a crackhead, right?"

"Yeah," he laughed. "Man, you junkies are real perceptive. And for the record, I prefer the term "Freebase cocaine user." Crackhead sounds so ... low budget. Although I am enjoying all the Valium they got here."

He stuck his tongue out and showed me a ten mg. tablet, made a coughing motion and palmed it for later. I had already been doing the same, so I could at least try and get loaded from taking three or four at once instead of dotted throughout the day. This guy, I really did peg for a junky.

Food came and went, but I couldn't hold anything down. The

anti-nausea drugs didn't work on me, but I've always had a bad stomach, even before the smack. A girl who worked when Jay had the day off immediately became the source of conversation between Todd and Billy. She was tall, dark skinned, covered in tattoos. Pretty, I suppose. They half-heartedly tried to include me in the banter but I was too out of it by this time, looped on my medication and two days into cold turkey. I lay back on my bed, and then curled into the foetal position, feeling more alone than I have ever felt as they laughed and guffawed among themselves.

I had moments of clarity in the early hours. I'd get up when the others were snoring softly and sit out by reception under the strip lighting. I'd talk to Jay about music, or rather he'd talk at me and I'd grunt in the affirmative or negative and drool. I liked the detox wing early in the morning. It was peaceful at least. The girl who worked there was called Alicia, and she talked to me about what I was going to do when I got out. I couldn't answer her. I didn't even want to talk about it. I was an illegal immigrant; I'd let the paperwork slide to such an extent when I was strung out that my temporary work permit was now expired by nine months. I had no place to live and no regular income. She asked me if I thought I could stay clean once I got out. I thought about it and in light of what I was coming out to, I answered in the negative. Again, she tried to press me on going over to the rehabilitation part of the building, but I repeated what I'd said before about being broke and she drifted off.

I woke up the next day with cuts around my wrists and up my arms. Crudely, the word *heroin* was etched into my forearm in scratchy red letters. It was actually Jay who noticed it when he woke me at seven to give me my medication. I reached out with my left hand and my shirt pulled up and Jay commented on them.

"When did you do this?" he asked.

"I honestly don't remember."

"Well, don't to it again or they'll section ya."

"Yeah. Let's get those pills."

The third and forth days were the worst. They blended into one endless fever dream where the sun rose and set randomly.

My meds were at their maximum level at this point, yet they could not stop the horrors and the physical agonies of my withdrawals. I awoke at three a.m. and listened to Billy and Todd sleeping. I flopped over in the sweatbox that was my bed and landed on the remote control. The TV flickered into life and *A Clockwork Orange* was on the screen in black and white. Alex was bellowing "I was cured all right!" when I managed to flick it off.

I sat with Alicia in the front desk in the early hours. I was signing papers in a headfog of Valium. An answer-phone light blinked at me with hypnotic regularity ...

"Lord, grant me the serenity to accept the things I cannot change ..."

Balmy Los Angeles evening. Crickets chirp as a warm wind blows in from the coast ...

"The courage to change the things I can,"

A voice with a soft West Coast lilt reciting some kind of prayer ...

"And the wisdom to know the difference."

And I am surfacing, upright in a plastic chair part of a circle of men in the twilight ...

"Amen."

I joined in with this, anticipating it in some primitive part of my brain. The meeting was over before it even started for me. Fuck, passing out in public again. How embarrassing.

But I was too stoned on Valium and sick to articulate any kind of apology. Nobody seemed to mind, anyhow. Somewhere in my back brain I realized that this must be the end of the fourth night. I should have been feeling better by now. Maybe I did.

My head cleared and the pain stopped gradually, in almost imperceptible steps. Two new men arrived, much older than the rest of us. The frailest of them looked heavily sedated and partially bedridden. First I spoke to Tommy, the other new arrival, a barrel-chested old man with weathered red features curved into a Victorian scowl, topped off with a white bushy handlebar moustache. Tommy was a drunk, and worked at sea his whole life. We were in the smoking garden sometime after breakfast. He was ill-looking and pale, still trembling slightly and telling me how they had to hospitalise him after an initial attempt to detox here because he started to have violent fits.

"Woke up in the hospital, stinking and sober, bruised up and bleeding, tongue half bit thru', with no idea of where I was, or why I was there."

Todd later introduced me to Sal; the frail-looking old man who peered at me over his round glasses, propped up in his bed. Sal was in his late sixties, and looked more like he should be in a care home than a detoxification ward. He blinked in recognition and wheezed an agonized breath.

"What are you coming off?" I asked him as he continued to study me. He looked as if he was thinking of the right thing to say to me. When he came to a decision, his face took on a look of quiet determination and he nodded his head. Sal leaned forwards, beckoned me over to him and grabbed my collar. He brought his lips over to my ear.

"Call my wife." he hissed. "Tell ... that... bitch ... to get me two ... TWO balloons ... and a spoon ..."

Then he fell back onto the bed and started muttering in agonized Spanish.

"Jesus," I said to Todd as we split to get our medication. "He's fucking looped on tablets. Either that or he's fucking senile."

"Yesterday he told me that he's here to kick smack and angel dust, if you can believe that. Says the last time he kicked was 1978."

That really was something. I could understand why they had medicated him so heavily. A sixty-something year-old man, coming off of a twenty-two year heroin and PCP bender—now that had to be painful.

After I received my pills from the nurse, a beady-eyed old white woman who looked at me like I was liable to cut her throat and abscond out of the window with her purse, Alicia beckoned me into her office.

"I've got some good news for you," Alicia said, sitting in her chair and motioning for me to take a seat. It reminded me of one of my old doctor's office back in England. The poster with the kitten hanging from a branch captioned, "Hang in there!" There was no stamp here of the personality that I'd imagined Alicia to have, nothing of the tattooed punk rock ex-junky at all. This could be the office of a fifty-something Christian charity worker. Again, my view of "sober people," as twelve-steppers like to refer to themselves, slipped further.

"I'm cured?" I joked, getting a smile out of her.

"Well, not quite. What would you say if I asked you to consider coming over to the rehabilitation wing after your detox is over?"

"I can't. I don't have dollar one, Alicia. I don't even know where I'm gonna sleep when I get out. Sorry."

"What if you didn't have to pay? You see, I put in an application for the Musicians' Assistance Program to pay for you to stay longer with us and the approval came through today. All you've got to do is sign here..."

She told me about the Musicians' Assistance Program as I sat pondering my next move. They had formed in the 70s, a group of sober survivors of the 60s from the LA music industry. They started off running a musicians-only AA meeting which proved to be hugely popular, attracting some pretty big players from the jazz era, as well as rock and roll groups and executives from many of the big record labels. After a number of high profile musicians died from fatal overdoses, MAP set up a trust which paid for musicians who couldn't afford it or didn't have insurance, to get access to treatment. The only requirement was that you had to have recorded on an album. I suppose it made sense; I thought that Alicia was taking an unusual interest in the bands I had been in, querying me about dates and record labels. And now she had gotten me a break with these MAP people.

The idea of staying here for thirty more days was terrifying to me. I knew that in this wing, we were treated with kid gloves because we were detoxing and fragile. But in the rehab wing, things would no doubt be far less relaxed. I knew people who had been to rehab; it always sounded to me like a prison for junkies, and only something that someone who had absolutely no choice in the matter would endure. I was due to be discharged the day after tomorrow. I had already planned out who I would call to pick me up, how much money I could borrow off of them, and when I could get my first taste for a week.

I listened to myself think this with a feeling of revulsion. Here I was considering leaving this place. Five days ago, I never wanted to shoot up again. I was fully aware that each day was creeping closer towards the only possible conclusion to my reckless drug use. I was desperate for a shot at rehab so I could get my life together. I was suicidal, a prisoner who lived in motels and on people's floors, someone covered in track marks and dirt that nobody—except the occasional out-of-it junky girls—would consider fucking. Twenty-two years old and fucked up, sick, broke, and alone. A miserable existence. Yet here I was, clean for the first time in almost two years, and I was already planning my first hit of smack for when I got out. And when something looked like it might come between myself and that hit, here I was ready to discard it. Discard 3,500 dollars of other people's money offered specifically for the purpose of giving me a chance at what I'd wanted without my even having to ask. Jesus, I was in trouble. I signed the papers quickly and said thank you to Alicia. She was positively beaming with pride. I knew that this was probably all her doing; Alicia must have had a soft spot for lame animals like myself.

I went back to my bed. In the next bunk, Todd was lounging around, flicking through a magazine. I told him what had happened and he seemed pleased; I would be graduating to the rehabilitation wing on the same day as him and Billy. He told me that he thought it would be easier to get through the month that way. He sounded like he was looking forward to it, almost.In the bed in the far corner, Sal slept in a Valium hush.

NEAR MISSES (Part Three)

I somehow ended up in Beverly Hills with Chris on some
harebrained scheme to get high. Chris had a look of quiet
desperation about him—he was out of drugs and soon he would
be out on the streets. His housemates had finally figured out who
had been removing all of the furniture from the place item by
item and selling it, and they were trying to evict him. His father
had finally realized that his son's sustained financial crisis was
due to a heavy dependence on heroin. The old man was
threatening to not only stop loaning Chris money, but also to cut
off his allowance completely, demanding that Chris move back in
with him and sort his life out. So here we were; heading over to
the old man's house, not so Chris could make an attempt to clean
up but so we could rob the place. Chris roped me into this whole
scenario with the promise of free drugs; his father was an
anaesthesiologist and reputedly something of a barbiturate
addict himself, and in exchange for driving him out to the house I
was promised first pass on any drugs we found.

His father was in San Francisco on a speaking engagement
and as we pulled into the driveway, Chris pointed out his father's
second car, a new-looking, black Mercedes-Benz.

"Look at that," he sneered, genuinely angered, "a fucking
second Mercedes sitting in the driveway and the old bastard is
giving me static over a lousy 900 dollars a month! Makes you
sick. Pull in here. Neighbours 'round here got their noses in each
others business, man ..."

We pulled into the darkened parking area and walked to the
front door. Chris slid his key in the lock, deactivated the alarm
and we went in.

It was a beautiful place, an expensive looking upright piano to
the left as you walked into the living room, flat-screen TV and a

great sound system, giving the place the look of an upper class bachelor pad.

Chris set to work in the bedroom, looking for cash and jewellery, and I hit the medicine cabinet. I discarded vitamins, heart tablets and haemorrhoid creams. Then I came across some tablets that looked interesting. Checking the packaging, it seemed that they contained barbiturates and codeine. They went into my pocket.

It took me a while to find Chris's father's medical bag. When I did it was something of a goldmine. I discovered syringes, a blood pressure machine, more tablets, a stethoscope and some lidocaine ampoules. Checking the pills I found something quite extraordinary. A bottle of Quaaludes; containing one and a half pills. Chris's father was in semi retirement, working as a consultant to one of the big hospitals in West Hollywood, and these pills had obviously been hanging around since the early eighties. Hoping that they were still potent, I pocketed them.

Chris reappeared from the bedroom, obviously having found what he was looking for.

"You finished? Let's get the fuck out of here."

"Yeah," I muttered, examining one of the ampoules. "You know anything about lidocaine? It's an anaesthetic, right?"

"I suppose so. Let's roll."

"Wait, wait ... I wanna shoot some of this. I think it's in the same family as cocaine."

"Oh, Jesus. Well, hurry up," he sighed, heading for the kitchen. "Just give me a yell when you're through doing that ugly shit."

Chris, as heavily strung out on smack as he was, had a curiously puritanical attitude towards injectors. I suppose it made him feel a little better to have someone he could feel superior to.

I mainlined half an ampoule of lidocaine and waited. Nothing seemed to happen, apart from a mild chemical taste in the back of my throat. I waited for a few moments before injecting the rest and calling Chris.

"What are you gonna do when your old man finds out?" I inquired as we pulled out of the driveway.

"I dunno," he answered dreamily. "Maybe he won't notice. He's loaded, right?"

I've since found out that mainlining lidocaine is an extremely bad idea. It can cause cardiac arrest, instant death … as we got back into Hollywood, I started feeling strange: heavy lidded, out of focus. We stopped at a red light on Franklin, behind a white SUV.

I woke up, moments after we shunted into the vehicle in front of us. I had passed out, chin slumping onto my chest, foot slipping off the break, causing the car to lurch forward into the rear of the vehicle in front of us. With Chris screaming at me, I jerked back into life. Some fat, white American woman was getting out of the SUV, screaming abuse at us, waddling over to the driver's window on heavy thighs, banging on the glass and screaming about whiplash and insurance. My legs where completely numb and I was laughing, disorientated, as Chris screamed, "You fucking stupid junky bastard!" at me, and I passed into blackness once more. Apparently Chris had to get out and scream at the woman to get the fuck away, starting to attract all kinds of unwelcome attention, and when she wouldn't, he aimed a few swift kicks at her and had to pull out his knuckleduster before she retreated back into her vehicle. I came around somewhat as Chris was shoving me over into the passenger seat and gunning the engine, and I heard him tell me, "You are one stupid cocksucker, man," as we sped towards safety…

REHABILITATION

I spent two more days convalescing in the detox ward. During the last twenty-four hours, my medication was reduced to zero. My short-term memory was shot to hell. A year and four months of constant, heavy heroin and cocaine use had played havoc with my brain. I could not hold onto people's names. I forgot what day it was. Drifting off to sleep when I could, I dreamed of the chaos of Iris Circle, Genesis naked bathed in lamplight, tarot cards spread out in a semi-circle in front of her, injecting crystal meth. My own needle, penetrating my gray flesh without so much as a sensation ... then I would jerk awake, gasping for air, expecting the rush to take me in its chemical grasp before stopping and taking in my surroundings with the sudden taste of disappointment. Sadly, I would close my eyes and try to recapture the feeling.

The morning I moved over into what the staff referred to as "population," I showered and cursed the way the water hurt my skin. Every inch of my body felt oversensitive. Any temperature apart from room temperature was unbearable to me. The air burned or froze me. The feel of my T-shirt fabric against my skin was profoundly unpleasant. I was in a near constant state of anxiety, worrying endlessly about where I was going to go, if I had warrants for my arrest waiting for me on the outside.

I packed up my clothes and my books, and was met by Sandra—the woman who had booked me in originally—who took me to the population wing. Before I was allowed in I was taken to a waiting area where my bag was taken to be searched for contraband. They eventually removed the books and a wife beater. I was given a slip for the three items to be redeemed when I left. The wife beater was out, they explained, because they have had trouble when people have spotted rival gang

157

tattoos on other clients. So now everyone had to wear T-shirt sleeves or longer. The books were out because I was forbidden to have any reading materials other than those which where linked to "recovery." My books were a copy of Burroughs's *Junky* and *The Hot Zone,* a book about an Ebola outbreak.

Next I was strip searched in a bare white room by a queer black kid who had "ex-prison bitch" inked all over him.

"OK, you good," he said, flashing a gold tooth at me and motioning for me to get dressed.

"I've just been in the detox wing for the past seven days. What the fuck you think I'm gonna have on me?"

"You'd be surprised, man, you'd be surprised," he grinned. "Or maybe not. You a junky after all, right?"

His name was Junior and it was eight in the morning when he led me up to my room. I vaguely hoped that I would be rooming with Billy and Todd who were moving over on the same day as me, as they seemed prettyokayfrom what I knew of them. I was disappointed then, when he introduced me to two odd-looking guys who straightened up like they where in military school when we knocked and walked in. They slumped again, upon seeing it was only Junior and myself.

"Hi, boys," Junior announced. "We got a new kid here."

My new roommates were Michael and Simon, two freakily mismatched men who immediately struck me as being a little off. Michael was in his late twenties, an overeager and over-friendly man who looked like an accountant on the skids. He called me "buddy" and shook my hand with a strong grip. Simon was older, with foppish sandy hair. He talked in a nasal camp whine, his false teeth whistling. His face was webbed with ruptured blood vessels, and his eyes had the ferocious sheen of a man who had seen the insides of mental wards and police cells and consequently, I liked him a little more than the other guy.

Junior excused himself, telling us to hurry it up, and Michael sneered, "Jesus, did he do your strip search? D'you have to fight him off?" as I unpacked my clothes. We rushed out to our morning meeting.

Turns out I wasn't far wrong in my assessment of Michael; he was a broker on the skids who had lost it to crack. I suppose it started off like a typical story: high pay, high-pressure job, engaged to his high school girlfriend, looking to buy a house. He used a bit of coke after work with the guys, mostly to fuel their drinking sessions. Michael liked coke, though, and he found it helped him to work better. He was more confident and aggressive on coke and in his line of work that was a bonus, so he started a routine of having a couple of lines before important meetings. Over a few years coke became essential to his being. He became gripped by terror at the thought of having to face the day without a couple of grams tucked away in his suit jacket. Only he was having to snort more and more, and his nose was fucked up. He was blowing out red matter all of the time, and getting nose bleeds during the night.

He was introduced to freebasing by his dealer's girlfriend who he had started fucking on the side. When that whole story came out, he lost his fiancée, and soon after lost his job. His habit was expensive to keep up, and he couldn't keep off of coke for more than a couple of days at a time. His last chance to salvage his career came when a large company offered him a job. It lasted a few months before he started again, and simply stopped turning up to work. He stayed in his apartment, sucking on the pipe and conducting paranoiac plays within his head in which the DEA were camped outside of his apartment, or where his ex-fiancée was fucking all of his friends, laughing about his coke-fuelled impotence. He got arrested for the first time trying to force his way into her apartment with a golf club. The second and third bust followed in quick succession.

The last arrest came at the very end of the line. Michael now had no source of income, was cut off from his family completely and getting by on unemployment checks. He was on Alvarado and 6th, trying to trade food stamps for crack. He spotted a guy working on a storefront, fixing a sign. The guy had popped inside of the shop for a moment, leaving his drill unattended. Michael did the calculations quickly and decided that he could get at least

159

forty dollars for the drill. He crossed over, trying to look inconspicuous. Then he grabbed the drill and ran.

Michael was a bad thief. You could tell just by looking at him—brazen, scared and desperate. A cry went up and before he knew what was happening, the owner of the drill and some of his friends were chasing him. They were bigger than him and gaining. At the intersection where 6th crosses Alvarado, he decided to run into traffic in a bid to lose his pursuers.

He ran, focusing only on the screams of the horns, the screech of tires and the yells of the guys who seemed only feet away. A motorcyclist swerved to avoid him, and as it did, with a thud, an SUV bounced him off of its bonnet. He flew backwards and landed in a heap, still holding the drill to his chest. Everything seemed to stop. He could hear sirens wailing in the distance although it seemed improbably early for the police to be there. He staggered to his feet and carried on running. He ran straight into an ambulance responding to a different emergency, which tossed him back to the tarmac with a crunch. A crowd was gathering now, but in his dazed and frightened state, Michael just wanted to keep running. He struggled to his feet. The last thing he remembered before waking up in the emergency room was the pain—an explosion of violent, terrible pain, as he put his weight on his right leg. He had a vague recollection of seeing his leg twist and give way, bending at an impossible angle before he collapsed to the ground again and shut down completely.

He was here on his father's insurance, hobbling around with a cane and pins through his leg in a last chance to avoid doing jail time. I didn't figure Michael would last in jail, and I suppose he knew it, too. He still had something of the All-American asshole about him; not even the crack had managed to take away that guileless cheerfulness. If he ended up inside I had no doubt that he would end up beaten into submission and gang fucked by everyone so inclined.

He was still inside when I checked out of rehab and could be there still for all I know. He wanted to become a drugs worker, and I hope it worked out for him because I had a feeling he would hit the pipe as soon as he hit the street despite all of the talk of it being over. He had that look in his eyes; the same one I had, the look of a pet dog that had just been beaten by its master—total paralysis by hurt, confusion and fear.

I spent the next twenty-eight days in the bizarre unreality of drug rehabilitation. Rehab is a place where you are thrown in with a variety of characters with whom you would normally have nothing more than a superficial connection. Latino gang members, crackhead lawyers, septuagenarian junkies, alcoholic priests, coke-crazed pilots—a whole world of strange, fringe characters who you are thrown together with … all of you sick and vulnerable without your security blanket of drugs or alcohol; trying to figure out how to get better, getting yelled at for not cleaning floors and toilets with the correct amount of vigilance by staff, sleeping in communal spaces, sharing intimacies of your life in group therapy sessions and compulsory Narcotics Anonymous meetings. I sat there during break times freezing in the ninety degree Pasadena heat, clutching my leather jacket closed and cursing the air conditioning inside the building. I met Richard, a slight man with a prosthetic leg who worked for the government in the early nineties painting military aircraft with a kind of experimental paint which it was later discovered gave seventy-five percent of the people working on the project a particularly aggressive form of cancer. They sued and the case dragged its way though the courts, the resulting ruling against the military coming too late for most of them who had succumbed to tumours and agonized last hours on morphine drips in sterile wards. Richard made it, though, gave evidence at a senate committee hearing, had his fifteen minutes of fame in the news media and accepted a settlement, with which he then used to drink himself almost to death. When I knew him he was ill, riddled with tumours and a cirrhotic liver. He was tortured, knowing that at forty-five he probably didn't have long to live with his body in such bad shape, torn between the desire to make his family proud of him for getting off of booze and a desire just to drink the pain away and live out whatever years or months he had left with at least the numbness of chronic alcoholism to take the edges off. He cried a lot, and called me the day his insurance ran out and they sent him back into the real world. I had only been out for three days myself. The last time I spoke to him he was in a bar, his voice tired and slurring, the sound of a TV playing some football game in the background. He was tired, he told me, and he was tired of living. He wanted me to meet him and bring him some sleeping pills. I told him to hang on, took the address, turned my phone off and never heard from him again. Where are you, Richard, three years and more on from then? Still waiting in some bar for the connection that will never arrive, still telling anyone who will listen about the government and how they screwed their own people leaving them to die, broken, like lab animals? Still crying, talking about the children you cannot see anymore, days on the beach in Santa Monica, cold beers and singsong laughter? Where are you Richard?

My caseworker was a nice guy, in his mid thirties. I met with him once a week for a one-on-one session and we talked about books mostly: Charles Bukowski, Burroughs, all the good stuff. He was an ex-speed freak who decided to quit shooting up when he found himself lying in the bath listening to voices gurgling out of the taps telling him he was about to die of a heart attack. Our sessions went around in circles though, as he tried to explain the theory of the twelve-steps to me. His insistence that I abstain from not only heroin but also all drugs and even alcohol led to several arguments. The very idea that someone can come into a place an addict and emerge from it not needing even the occasional joint or beer to take the edge off was—and still is— ludicrous to me. I also had other doubts about the whole twelve-step recovery program. Coming from an Irish Catholic background, I had more than my fill of religions for one lifetime.

Despite everybody's protests to the contrary, the program did seem very much like a religion to me, with its talk of God, its prayers, and its semi-mysticism. During meetings I often heard people insist that you should only spend time with other people "in the program." I imagined myself hanging out with a bunch of bible bashing ex-dopers and drinkers for the rest of my life and I laughed. Better I joined the Scientologists—at least I might get

162

to hang out with John Travolta. Often at the end of meetings, people would stand, hold hands and recite the Lord's Prayer. Their "get out clause" to the accusation that AA was a religion was that the "God" referred to in the twelve-step texts was a "God of your own understanding." So why did I find myself holding hands with people and reciting the Lord's Prayer? "That kind of attitude," they told me, "is why you can't stay off of drugs". I told my caseworker that I wanted to get off heroin, but I wanted to do it my way. No meetings, no total abstention from all drugs, just a bit of discipline and self-control. He laughed, made me hold out my arms which where literally covered in bruises, fresh track marks, lumps and razor slashes and asked me how much faith I had in my discipline and self control. I suppose he had me there.

One day he asked me to write why I felt that I had needed heroin in the past, and why I thought that it may be difficult to stay away from it in the future—a concept known as "relapse prevention." Here is some of what I wrote:

From the day we are born we are forced to submit to completely false and ridiculous institutions such as school, the state, god, police, government, work, the idea of being a good citizen, (as if that means anything), marriage, wholesomeness and a moral code. All of this imposed on us down the years by the kind of conservative, church loving assholes who have made this world the farce it is for as long as we have had a concept of society. This is because these same people need a stupid and complaint society to continue to work and pay taxes, fight their wars and fund their lifestyles. This is a completely unnatural state of affairs and creates a kind of mass existential / spiritual crisis, a collective mental illness. This manifests itself in riots, murders, suicide and war. I choose to deal with it by shooting dope. It's either that, or commit a mass murder.

He didn't like that, and told me this wasn't a philosophy class, it was a chance to change my life. He told me to "Let go and let God." More bullshit catchphrases, and on it went.

Evenings were the best, as we got to leave the compound to

attend outside meetings. Split into groups of twenty, our minibus journeyed across town to meetings in social clubs, churches and basements all over the city: Pasadena, Hollywood, East L.A., and Boyle Heights. The meetings themselves were a drag, but driving through the city at night wasn't. For all of us it was the highlight of the day. Many of the men I shared the ride with had been in there for months, others coming straight here from long stretches in prison on possession or supply charges. We were grown men, pressing our noses against the glass, looking at the city like country bumpkins in the big smoke for the first time as we drove past old bars and scoring spots, crossing by Hollywood and Vine and me inhaling long and smooth as if I could somehow breathe in the fumes from the crack being sold here and smoked in public bathrooms and darkened doorways.

I heard terrible stories in those meetings of lives ruined and families split apart. A guy from a wealthy Jewish East Coast family whom I had gotten to know pretty well in the compound shocked me by telling his story of a meth - induced breakdown in LA during one of these outside meetings. He was trying to score a large quantity of crystal days before he was due to attend his father's funeral in New York. In the insanity that followed he ended up ripping off a dealer and staying in the Tropicana Motel off of Sunset, shooting as much of it as his heart could stand before freaking out and calling the cops, telling them that he was insane and going to kill himself. He was taken from the motel babbling speed induced nonsense in a stretcher and stuck under 72 hour suicide watch in the charity ward of an LA bughouse where he observed patients jerking off and throwing their cum at staff, people shitting themselves and pissing their pants constantly, a girl chasing invisible butterflies. When the crank wore off he was broke, had missed his father's funeral and was given a bus token to get back into Hollywood. Shaking and still withdrawing, he shit his only pair of pants during the bus ride and finally called his family collect to discover that he was to be cut out of the inheritance unless he checked into rehab. And that was how he arrived at the front desk, penniless and stinking with pants full of crap.

164

A number of people dropped out or were thrown out while I stayed there. One kid I had been in a group therapy session with, who had told everyone how he liked to torture animals, especially dogs, finally freaked out and walked out of the main entrance to score some speed. Defaulting on treatment meant that he would be sent back to jail, but at that point I suppose he didn't care. Another guy who had been there for six months before I arrived and was now able to leave in the day time and attend work was busted smoking heroin in his room and thrown out. Billy freaked after two weeks and walked out, announcing his intention to buy a bottle of whiskey and a rope, get drunk and hang himself. All around me it seemed that the problems were incurable, and that maybe one or two percent of us stood any chance of making it. The smart money was not on me being one of the privileged few.

Dee-Dee even left, in a manner. He was the head guy there, a skinhead in his late forties with a walrus-like moustache and swastikas tattooed on either side of his neck. He had a neat round scar in his throat where a tube was inserted to keep him breathing after one of his various near death experiences. He was incredibly skinny; slight of stature, yet had the whole place scared of him. I'm not sure why, but everybody just seemed to understand that you didn't fuck with Dee-Dee. He led a meeting once, telling us a little about his background. He was a member of some white supremacist group in the late sixties and spoke about the whole period with a world-weary kind of sadness. Sadness for the fact that he was so young and stupid and naive believing the bullshit that he did, sadness for the way the sixties ended bringing in an era of increasing repression and tough consequences for his peer group and sadness for watching his friends die, one after the other, while he held on despite his best efforts. He was ill, suffering from AIDS and no longer as strong as he used to be. His reign came to an end before I left that place. He became too ill to be involved in the day-to-day running of the rehab and faded into a less intense role, though haunting the building still with his hawk-like features.

I left rehab after twenty-eight days with 500 dollars in my pocket and nowhere to go. I checked into a short let motel in

Pasadena and settled down to wait. I was healthier, my arms were healing up and three meals a day had put some weight on me. I contacted a few people who I trusted and told them I was over my recent troubles and ready and willing to work again. I got drunk on the first night, buying a bottle of Southern Comfort and some orange juice. I sat by the pool at the motel and watched the stars, polishing off the whole bottle. It was a beautiful night and I got blissfully, happily drunk. When the bottle was done, I smiled to myself, pleased that I had gotten good and drunk and the sky hadn't fallen in. In rehab, everyone had given me the impression that having been a heroin addict I could never drink in a normal way again, that even one beer would inevitably begin a downward spiral which would leave me back on the street with a syringe buried into the crook of my arm. But here, by the pool of a Holiday Inn in Pasadena I was drunk and happy and the world seemed OK.

The next day, walking around Pasadena I found a bus that ran all the way to East Hollywood. Without thinking I got on it, with forty dollars in my pocket. By seven that evening and almost without realizing I had done it, I was back in the hotel room, with four needles from the exchange, two rocks of crack and a bag of dope. This time was different though, I told myself. This time I wouldn't get hooked.

CORPUS DELICTI

I was hanging out by the mouth of the back alley running behind the apartment building from which Carlos's replacement Macho operated. I would sometimes see reoccurring characters lurking around just like me. Just like me they seemed to be rendered in black and white against the color and brightness of the Los Angeles mid-afternoon sunlight. Just like me they sniffled and coughed and tried to look nonchalant, returning often to the pay phone to page their connections again and again. They sucked dejectedly at sodas or beers from the 7-11 on the corner, or sometimes just sat with their heads in their hands and waited for their guy to show up.

The car was gone. Pawned for 100 dollars at an auto-pawn place downtown. I sat there, sick and hopeless shortly following my relapse. In a matter of weeks my habit was back, stronger than before. On a muted TV screen in the waiting room, while the old black lady behind the bullet-proof glass processed my payment and generated a pawn slip, I watched a Concorde burn in furious reds and oranges upon a Paris airstrip. Black smoke belched and vomited up into the sky. I looked at my arms, covered in gooseflesh and bloody, angry red injection sites. The action on screen suited my mood, perfectly.

I noticed a new girl at the pay phone that afternoon, a few months after leaving rehab when I was back to scoring day after day, back to a state of pure need and desperation. I had no more been able to control my use of heroin and crack than I was able to control my use of oxygen. I was grimly following a path of total obliteration, and once I had given up and let go of my niggling thoughts of staying clean, of getting into the twelve-step programme, of struggling though life without heroin to ease the ache in my soul, I felt a palpable sense of relief. I was now an athlete totally focused on the goal of total oblivion at all times. A star racehorse. A heavyweight champion.

Physically, the girl looked like a survivor of Dachau, bone thin legs in black tights with a black miniskirt wrapped around a barely-there ass and waist. She was on the pay phone, facing away from me, smoking a cigarette and punching numbers. The outline of her rib cage was clearly visible under a skin tight, long-sleeved, dirty grey top which exposed one pitiful shoulder, entirely free of muscle or fat. On top of that torso sat a dirty mop of blonde hair which made her head look far too big for her body. She looked as if she would shatter into her component pieces if she tripped over her rickety high-heels and hit the concrete.

I sensed someone's approach, heard a whistle and there was Macho, dressed down in a Lakers top and sweat pants, loitering by the mouth of the alleyway. I got up and walked towards him, along with the apparition in black from the pay phone. It seemed that we were both Macho's clientele.

He turned back down the alleyway and we followed like children begging their father for money or candy.

"Whatchoo need, whatchoo need?" he hissed.

"Forty," I replied.

"Twenty," I heard the girl cough out from behind me.

He stopped and moved his tongue around his mouth to separate out the different sizes of balloons as I handed him the money. The girl was beside me now as she handed over the cash and I caught a faint sickly-sweet smell of body odour and junk-sickness wafting from her. Raphael turned and dispensed the medication into our eager hands.

"Haff a nie-ce daye," he grinned in mangled English, before turning and walking away.

"Spick cocksucker," the girl muttered in a faraway voice.

I turned and looked at her ravaged face. Her skull stuck out through her skin like the modernist angles of a Picasso portrait. Her lips were swollen and cut. Her eyes were heavy lidded and dead certainly, but there was no denying that I knew this girl.

168

"Genesis?" I asked quietly.

We walked together for a while, through the side streets and back alleys to find the spot where she said we could get high. We didn't talk much. She explained the lip had happened after some *"fucking asshole nigger"* had refused to pay for head. I walked in silence mostly, my eyes returning to her wasted body, unable to comprehend the ruin the girl had visited upon herself in the period following her overdose in my apartment.

We soon came upon an abandoned blue Volvo in an overgrown lot hidden from view by chain-link fences. She opened the back door, sending the concentrated heat and stench from inside steaming out into the desert air and said, "Get in."

Inside we cooked our dope in silence. The smell filled the car, drowning out the smell of dust, rotting food and stale sweat. Empty wrappers from bags of heroin and coke lay across the floor, along with discarded fast food containers—Jack In The Box, El Pollo Loco, Burger King, Arby's ...

I had to loosen my jeans to get to the vein which had been working recently, a long blue one running up the outside of my left thigh. I noticed Genesis rolling her top down, exposing one white tit to the daylight. I watched her silently as she appraised her breast in the same way that a butcher might examine a fresh piece of meat for imperfections. Then finding her spot she squeezed the flesh hard with her left hand and slowly slid the needle in, checking for a working vein.

I returned to my own shot and fed the heroin into my bloodstream slowly, careful not to damage the vein. I withdrew the needle and looked over at Genesis. She had withdrawn the needle and was reinserting in a different spot. She noticed me watching.

"It's the goddamn crank," she explained. "Fucks up your veins real quick. Who knows what those bastards mix it with. I've been getting some joy here recently but ..."

She froze as a small plume of blood shot up into the barrel.

"Gotcha," she breathed.

She finished up and with a cursory wipe of the injection site with the back of her grimy hand she popped her bloody breast back into her shirt. She lay back and closed her eyes in rapture.

For now, we were elsewhere. The silence stayed in the car for a long time.

"I'm sorry I left you," I told her eventually when the talk resumed. "You know, that night in the apartment. I panicked. I was all fucked up. I didn't know what to do."

She just laughed. The dimensions of her face had changed so much that her front teeth seemed bigger now, almost goofy. I could only see traces of the old Genesis who had once been a beautiful girl, fucked up, but beautiful. Now there was nothing left but a shell and the narcotics which kept it operating.

"Thass cool honey," She laughed, her voice taking on a slower and deeper tonality as the heroin took hold of her. "You did what you had to do. I'm sorry I trashed your place."

We returned to a stoned silence for a moment, before Genesis retrieved a pipe from her purse and started preparing to smoke some meth. She heated the bulb and rolled the pipe back and forth, the thick white chemical smoke filling the glass and sending puffs out of the hole in the top of the bulb, before she sucked it in, rolling the pipe to keep the meth in liquid form and keep the smoke coming. She handed me the pipe and I accepted.

"Can I ask you a question, though?" she said eventually.

"Sure."

"Did you screw me? You know, when I was out?"

I took my hit and looked at her in a kind of stoned disbelief. The ringing in my ears from the speed subsided a little before I replied, "Jesus, no. Why would you say that?"

"Ah, you're a guy, you know? But that's what I figured. I didn't hurt down there when I woke up, but I just wanted to be sure. You could tell me, you know? I wouldn't be mad after all this time."

I shook my head mutely and looked at her. Her face lit up suddenly and she smiled at me.

170

"Hey listen," she said, "I'm a little short today ... I normally charge 20 for this, but you want head? How much have you got?"

"Shit, Genesis I don't know about that." I looked out of the grimy windshield at the dirty sky and realized that it was time to go. I started to gather my drugs and my equipment up, slipping them into my pocket, "I only have five bucks and I need it to get back to Hollywood."

Then Genesis opened her mouth and reached in. She grabbed her front row of teeth on the top and with a little tug dislodged them. The false teeth came out, explaining the difference I had noticed earlier, and she leaned towards me, her ruined face suddenly aged another twenty years by the four-tooth-gap on the top row, and she whistled, "five isokayhoney, that'll do fine."

"Aw fuck, Genesis," I told her, "I'm sorry. I gotta go."

I stumbled out of the abandoned car.

"Aw *shit* man," she spat, "that's a real pain in the ass. Now I gotta go out on the street again today! Can you lend me the five?"

I really couldn't afford it but I pulled five singles out of my pocket and handed them to her. She gripped it hard in her tiny fist and said, "Thanks".

"Look," I said, "I'll see you around."

"For sure"

I started walking back towards where I could catch the bus heading west. I never saw her again.

GHOST TOWN

Six months on, spun out on crack, heroin and crystal meth
once more, stinking and weak, homeless and friendless, I tried to
quit again. I was too scared to return to the apartment I had
been renting on Blackburn Avenue because of a crazy stunt I had
pulled the night before. I let a dealer named Shakespeare crash
there with a girl he was screwing in exchange for a couple of
rocks of crack. When my crack was gone, I snuck into the living
room where he was passed out and took the rest of his stash,
which I guessed correctly was in his shoe. I took that back to my
room and smoked it compulsively, growing ever more paranoid
that he would wake up and discover what I had done. To make
matters worse, I knew that his uncle was involved in a gang
called El M and that this act of stupidity would not go
unpunished. I stuffed my clothes into a holdall and abandoned
the apartment at six in the morning, cracked out and insane with
fear while they slept on.

I hadn't paid rent in two months and realized that eviction
proceedings must surely be underway by now, anyway. I needed a
place to stay and a chance to get through the worst of my cold
turkey.

The guesthouse I ended up crashing in was located at the
back of a friend's house, in an area of Venice known locally as
Ghost Town. It was a slum area with a thriving crack scene and
what seemed like no apparent sources for heroin whatsoever. The
couple who had let me take over their guest room for a few weeks
were quite well-off, worthy and well intentioned, although I was
rapidly getting sick of their concerns about my health. Broke and
scared, I called them up telling them that I was trying to come
off of heroin again but couldn't do it in Hollywood. They offered
me the guesthouse as a place to stay while I got through the

worst of the physical symptoms and I accepted gratefully. Three days after arriving there I realized that—yet again—I did not have the strength or endurance to get through the next few weeks cold turkey. I needed to get heroin somehow, so that night I hit the street trying to score.

For a junky, the place really was a ghost town. At first I got excited when I walked around—on virtually every street corner guys loitered, whistling at cars as they cruised past, running up to the vehicles which pulled up and making sales. In dark corners, pressed against walls like statues, ebony figures appraised the foot traffic in the area. Some kids used laser pointers in what seemed to be a code to warn of approaching cops. Shabbily dressed buyers tried to hawk boom boxes, jewellery and other shit in exchange for drugs. I stepped over an older white guy who had obviously just been jacked for money, drugs or both. He was lying face down on the street, the back of his head smashed open and raw. It was a street-dealing scene almost as busy as Macarthur Park. However, after hitting the first three guys I came up to and getting offered nothing more than crack or PCP, I started to get a sinking feeling. I only had forty dollars on me, and in my sick state my overriding need was for heroin, not substitute drugs.

I finally found an old looking crack head skulking around the darker recesses of a basketball court on Rose. He watched me approach with a smirk. There weren't too many white kids walking around this area so late at night. He had me pegged for a junky straight away.

"Hey," I said as I walked towards him.

"Hey yourself," he replied with a voice so deep it was almost subliminal. "You looking for someone?"

"Look, I need to score man. I'm looking for chiva. Dope. You know where I can get some?"

"Chiva?" the old guy whistled. "You in the wrong place. All rocks around here, son. I can do you a good deal on some rocks ..."

"Listen, I'm a junky and I'm sick. All I'm looking for is dope."

174

"Well," the old guy said thoughtfully, "you're gonna be a looking motherfucker then, 'cos ain't no market for that round here. People want rocks, they come here. People want that shit they go downtown."

I thanked him and walked back to the guesthouse. It was eleven at night and I had no car. I was screwed. I went back to bed, took five 10milligram Valiums and tried to sleep.

The night seemed endless. As the sleeping pills took hold, I managed to fall into a drugged half sleep for a couple of hours, but by 2:30 in the morning I was wide awake again, wet with junk sweat, and doubled over with stomach cramps. I watched the sun rise on the wall of my room, checking the clock every ten minutes, convinced an hour must have passed by now. I vomited continuously into the trashcan by my bed, even when my stomach was empty, still having to lean over and regurgitate burning yellow stomach acid ever so often.

I called Raphael as soon as the clock hit eight. He seemed surprised to hear from me, and even more surprised when I told him where I was staying. He told me that he'd figured I'd gotten busted or OD'd, so I filled him in on what had been happening. I asked him for a twenty dollar bag of smack and he reluctantly agreed to drive it out to me. He always bitched when I wanted less than half a gram delivered, but I was insistent. I gave him detailed directions and he told me he'd be here at 9:30. I agreed to meet him a few blocks away and I settled down to wait.

This was the beginning of my third day without dope. Stomach cramps were increasing in their ferocity and all of my demons where coming to the surface, lurking under the bed and in the closet ... again I became totally aware of my situation, of the utter hopelessness of where I was and what I was about to do. I get 20 dollars worth of smack and then what? When it runs out, I am back to where I started ... less money, starting my kick all over again. A black chasm of despair opened up inside of me. A month in detox and rehab and here I was, six months later strung out worse than ever, out of money, sleeping in the guesthouse of some people I barely know. None of my friends from before I got a habit wanted to know me. So much time had passed since my last success with a band that I had faded totally from the collective consciousness; everyone who worked for our band at the label had moved on, no one remembered. Back in Britain I'd hear about what the others where doing—Laura working in TV and Radio, John had a single reviewed in the NME, Martine and Eloise had a new band and were signed to a record label. And here I was, stuck in this shithole area of Venice, dope sick and agonized, about to extend my misery for one more afternoon of tranquillity, stuck on the other side of the world from my old friends, my old life.

I was miserable. I wanted this to stop; I really wanted it to stop. I didn't just want a break from the drugs; I wanted to go back to before I stuck a needle in my arm for the first time, before I knew how fucking amazing that feeling is, before I blew it for myself by getting a taste of what heaven must feel like. How could I go back to blissful ignorance now? Despite the dire situation I was now in and how unhappy it made me, I knew that the sad truth was that being straight, getting out of bed and starting the day without a shot of dope just wasn't a possible reality for me anymore. How could I live with the horrors and the boredom of being alive without something to make me feel that it was worthwhile, something to make me feel connected to the world around me? I'd changed. I'd altered my brain chemistry, my reward system my entire outlook on life, and as far as I could see the change was irreversible. I had no more control over what happened next than I had over the wind or the rain. I was at my habit's mercy.

It was late morning when my phone finally went off. I had lain there, squirming and cursing, puking and spitting, staring at the impertinent mute thing, willing it to buzz into life, to no avail. I had actually started to sleep when the phone did go off, and I snatched it up before the first ring had ended. Raphael's voice was the most beautiful thing I had ever heard at that moment and I gasped, "On my way," before hanging up.

I got up wearing only jeans and a T-shirt, no shoes, no socks. I had a sense of purpose now, like a long distance runner beginning his journey. I was focused totally on the transaction, on getting to Raphael as soon as possible, and then getting back so I could obliterate my feelings for another few hours. All those hours in rehab, sitting cross legged in a circle, concentrating on breathing and trying, unsuccessfully, to achieve the kind of spiritual peace though meditation that I am suddenly bestowed with while going to score. Maybe this is the closest I am ever going to get to that kind of bliss. My situation is suddenly cropped and reduced down to the bare essentials—I will leave, I will score, I will get high. Beyond that the world is an irrelevancy.

I left the house, nervously fingering the scrunched up twenty in my pocket. As soon as I had walked a couple of steps down the block, the heat rising from the pavement started to burn the soles of my feet. Well, fuck it. I considered the delay that returning to the guest house for a pair of shoes would entail and, deciding against it, I turned left on Rose and carried on walking the seven or eight blocks to where I was due to meet Raphael. The sidewalk changed from broken paving slabs to tarmac and the tarmac was beginning to melt already under the desert sun. I could feel its softness under my feet and became aware that it was beginning to stick to them. Each step became more and more painful. I could feel blisters forming, and I started to try and walk on the sides of my feet to take some of the pressure off my burning soles. The sun beat down mercilessly, but I fixed my mind on the drugs I was going to buy. Like some old Indian yogi walking on hot coals, the thought of fixing put the thoughts of my breaking and blistering flesh to the back of my mind.

I made it to a strip mall on the corner of Rose and Lincoln consisting of a Chinese take away, check cashing place, pawn shop and a laundromat. I ducked into a shaded spot and sat on the wall waiting for Raphael to show. I watched every passing car, intently looking for his face behind the wheel of his junkyard Toyota. A new-looking SUV pulled into the lot and I was surprised to see Raphael behind the wheel with a new girlfriend. I wondered absently if he'd finally stopped drinking and snorting and whoring every dollar he made.

I limped over and slid into the cool, air-conditioned vehicle. I closed my eyes, enjoying the feel of the leather seats and the cool air. I couldn't help but notice our change of circumstances. When I first met Raphael he was working the corner of Pico and Coronado in ripped sneakers, hustling for a dollar. I had a car, an apartment and a life. And now here I was, broke and broken, climbing into his new, air-conditioned ride.

"Hey buddy," Raphael grinned, turning round to face me. "You don't look so good."

His girlfriend turned to look at me and turned away just as quickly with a slightly disgusted look on her face. She muttered something in Spanish and started fixing her lipstick.

"I don't feel so good, my friend"

We did the deal and Raphael dropped me on the corner of my street. I thanked him, told him I'd be in touch, and split with my drugs. There's not a lot of small talk to be done between a dealer and a customer once the transaction is completed. If only all human interactions were so clean cut and defined.

I carefully slid the front gate open, and walked back into the house. Standing in the yard and watering the plants was Jim, one of the people who took me in this time. He looked up at me and raised an eyebrow.

"Hey, what you doing up? I thought you'd be ... well, you know."

Jim was in his fifties and had been on the periphery of the music industry for most of his life. He made his living training corporations to make more money by employing some kind of new age psychobabble that he tried to explain to me once, but my overriding impression of him was the bitterness he carried around at never making it as a musician. Maybe this is why he still tolerated me coming around to borrow money that I could never pay back, asking for a place to stay when things were bad. He probably thought of me as a colourful character and I was sure I made a funny topic of conversation when he hung out with his friends. I knew I was some kind of attempt to hang on to his past in the rock industry and it made me feel like a whore and a loser. Instead of sucking his cock I was here to be a performing monkey, to fit into some stereotype of an artist on the ropes. An artist who hadn't done anything more than shoot up for the past two years. Jim smoked pot and claimed to understand my problems, yet he thought it was as easy as just putting the needle down for me to get straight. Right now I was not in the mood for his homilies.

"Yeah, I'm not feeling so good. Tried to take a walk to clear my head but I didn't get far." I gestured to my bare feet. "Too hot to go more than a block without shoes."

"I'll say!" he laughed with mock concern. "You look pretty bad. You are doing the right thing, though. That shit will kill you, know what I'm saying?"

I stared right through him, focusing on getting past him, into the guesthouse and fixing.

"You're right, Jim. I'm over it. I just need to get my strength back and I'll be cool."

"Good, man." He gave me a friendly tap on the shoulder and I tried not to recoil from it. "Keep it up"

I walked past him thinking FUCK YOU JIM, FUCK YOU FUCK YOU, but saying something about going for a lie-down as I slipped inside my room to get myself well again. I split the twenty bag in two and shot into my neck for the sake of speed. I was shaky and weak and the idea of finding a vein anywhere else in a hurry seemed pretty remote. The shot instantly flooded my system with good feelings. I didn't get very high, but a familiar warmth radiated within me. A feeling of coming home.

I spent the day in a pleasant state of blessed out lethargy. Suddenly I had an interest in TV, music, writing again. I scribbled in my journal a little, ate some cakes and chocolates from the fridge, dozed off for a while. I awoke some time later, when the sun had set and something dark had risen in my heart. I looked at my pathetic wrap of smack and resisted the urge to do it. I wasn't sick yet. Again, the thought of what would happen when I ran out surfaced and I felt a pang of psychosomatic withdrawal symptoms simply from thinking about it.

I stood up with a new sense of purpose. I started hunting around for the last of my money, as always figuring the best way to not think about my situation. I was going to get high, and if there was no heroin in Ghost Town then I suppose I'd have to smoke crack. I rustled up forty dollars in bills and change and headed out of the back door.

An hour later and I sat with Henry and Arturo, two members of a street gang called the V13 (V for Venice, 13 for the thirteenth letter of the alphabet which is M for Mexico). I was cooking up a rock of crack in lemon juice sourced straight from the lemon tree growing out the back of the guest house and they watched me with mounting horror as I cooked it up, filtered it into a syringe and started digging for a vein.

"Man, shooting crack," Henry grumbled, shaking his head and looking at the floor, "that's some prison shit right there."

Henry was a man mountain; a local crack dealer covered in jailhouse and gang tattoos, and so it seemed absurdly comical that the sight of my cooking up and injecting crack shocked him. I smirked for a second before returning to the job at hand, which was focusing my attention on finding a suitable vein. As I pushed the concoction into a vein it stung—lemon juice is caustic, especially when administered intravenously. The hit was good. That familiar rush of adrenalin that comes from shooting coke took me and after glazing over for a moment, I came back to the situation at hand.

Earlier on I had scored a rock off Henry and took it back to the guesthouse. I didn't have a pipe, so I picked a lemon from out the back and injected the rock. I licked it first and as it tasted like coke, not soap or wax, I felt somewhat reassured about shooting it. The rush was good, so I headed out with the rest of my money to buy some more.

Henry talked a little more this time. He asked me if I was new to the area, if I lived nearby. I told him that I was two blocks away and he made me an offer. If he and his homeboy Arturo could come back to my place and have a smoke they would provide the pipe and a few free rocks. I was pretty looped on crack so I decided that this was a fine idea and Henry gave a coded whistle summoning Arturo, a dealer ensconced on a further street corner over. Introductions were made and we all headed back to the guesthouse. As Henry and Arturo made a bong out of a glass stem, some gauze and a soda bottle, I prepared a fix.

The pipe went round a few times, with the usually intensity of a crack session with strangers. Conversation was stilted and forced, and tended to drift off as we watched each other load the pipe and take a hit with starving eyes. Things only relaxed when the pipe was in my hand and I could concentrate on putting a rock on the gauze, holding a light to the stem, filling my lungs with the smoke, bellowing out plumes of white cocaine fumes, feeling the rush dizzying me and almost as quickly starting to fade as I passed the pipe on and resumed watching intently and awaiting another turn.

Pretty soon the crack was gone and Arturo turned to me.

"Let's go for a drive," he said. "We gotta pick up some more."

Cruising the back streets of Ghost Town, Henry at the wheel with Arturo lighting a joint laced with angel dust and me in the back seat, I started to get a bad feeling. My adrenalin was pumped up to insane levels and my guts churning in anticipation of something indefinable yet terrifying. Henry was circling a block with a set of projects on it shadowed with palm trees and whispering conspiratorially with Arturo. The joint was passed back to me but I refused it as the very smell of PCP was making me feel sick. I kept my eyes firmly on the guys in the front seat and my hand on the door handle in case I needed to bail out.

There was a kid hanging out on the corner and upon noticing him Henry whispered, "Here we go," killing the lights and turning into a side street half a block up from the kid. I watched as Arturo pulled a gun and a balaclava out of the glove box and slid the balaclava over his head, sticking the piece in his jacket pocket. I kept quiet. Silently he opened the car door, and slipped off into the night.

"What the fuck is he going to do?" I hissed to Henry after Arturo is gone.

"A debt. That nigger workin' the corner is getting jacked, man. Fucking pussy."

The silence of the night hung all around us in the balmy air. I heard the crackle of the pot burning as Henry took a drag. The chemical smell from the angel dust filled the car. I kept an eye on the street around us but it seemed completely deserted.

Suddenly, Arturo turned the corner, still wearing his balaclava and slumped into the passenger seat. Henry gunned the engine and we took off back towards the guesthouse. I watched Arturo place the gun back in the glove box, and even in the dark I could see it was slick with blood.

"Here, cop this," Arturo told me, as he shoved something back towards my hand. I opened my palm and he dumped a bloody mess into it. In the red goop were seven or eight cellophane wrapped rocks and one smashed front tooth. I brushed the tooth to the floor with a shudder and closed my fist around the drugs.

"Watch the blood there," Arturo told me dryly. "I had to knock the shit out of the jungle-bunny's mouth."

LEAVING LOS ANGELES

Jim and Sheila left for Sheila's mother's house in Orange County early the next day. They would be gone for the day, returning the following morning. My attempt to withdraw was already out the window. They thoughtfully left the keys for me and remarked that I looked like I was over the worst of it before leaving me to my own devices.

It took me fifteen minutes to find money in the house, collecting forty dollars in singles and fives. Raphael showed up around three to drop off more dope and I started my routine all over again. As soon as it was dark, Henry and Arturo showed up with some rocks and a pipe, looking to hang out. Looking back I can see the move they were pulling on me with shocking clarity. I was so high and so blinded by the offer of free crack that I remained completely unaware to the end.

It all happened at around three in the morning.

It was a long, surreal night. I had been smoking massive amounts of crack with Arturo and Henry and riding around with them while they made sales through the passenger windows of other vehicles or in darkened street corners. By three I was jittery and alone, parked a block and a half away from the guesthouse. They had told me to wait, as they were going to buy some weight having sold all of their rocks over the previous five hours and that they might be a while. They left a decent sized rock in the car and told me to smoke and wait. I had been there for twenty minutes when I noticed some crazy guy off in the distance; shirt off, doing push-ups in the middle of the street. The yellow streetlights glinted off his body as he moved up and down with a lizard-like deliberation. I loaded the pipe and took another hit, listening to the crackle of the rock and enjoying the taste as I blew out a white cloud of crack smoke. I wanted to get back to the guesthouse.

Suddenly I was gripped by the urge to leave Henry and Arturo here and run back there, refusing to answer their knocks. I was bored of this game, I was paranoid and edgy and I wanted my solitude so I could enjoy a good hit of smack and sleep, letting the poisonous crack work its way out of my system. My gaze fell on the crazy guy doing push-ups once more, my paranoia creeping up on me further as I noticed his face tipped in my direction. Was he watching me?

I don't know how long I sat there stupefied by the crack before I realized what was going on. When I did realize, I dashed out of the car, slamming the door shut, and I ran as fast as I could, chest burning and breath tearing out of me in great gasps, back to the guest house which had, of course, been robbed by Henry, Arturo and no doubt others, who were all since long gone. They had taken all of the expensive computer equipment in the place: printers, scanners, Macs, as well as a television set. I surveyed the damage in dumb shock, before checking in my bag to retrieve a needle. I sat in the bathroom listening to the buzz of the light for a while, cooking up my shot and thinking.

After my shot, at last a sense of calm descended upon me and I was able to make decisions. I thought it would be prudent to report the robbery first thing in the morning so it didn't seem so strange that I was out when it happened. A trawl around the guesthouse revealed the robbers had overlooked an expensive looking tool set, which I left to the side before going to bed. I lay and drifted for a few hours, stoned and somewhat more content.

In the morning I walked over to a pawnshop I had spotted on my way over to Jim's place, and pawned his tools for a hundred dollars. Then I returned to the house and dialled 911.

The cops were at the guesthouse taking notes when Jim and Sheila arrived back. I could sense that they knew something wasn't right but that they couldn't say anything to me, so I decided it was best that I left as soon as possible.

It was almost Christmas and I decided I could no longer carry on. I was out of luck, out of veins, out of dignity and out of money. I knew I had to leave Los Angeles.

I kicked in the Motel Deville in East Hollywood, a place were I used to score crack in the parking lot. I called my parents and told them I wanted to come home for Christmas, and begged them to send me a ticket. Within twenty-four hours my flight was arranged—I was to leave in one week, to arrive in London December twentieth. I turned my phone off upon receiving the news and settled down to wait out the rest of my withdrawal.

It was the sickest I can remember being. For six days and nights I burned with a fever, suffered migraines so severe that I literally screamed in agony. Stomach cramps doubled me over and I vomited everything I tried to eat. I had filled the room with bottled water and tins of soup prior to finishing the last of my heroin and I survived on these, leaving my bed only to use the bathroom. With the curtains drawn, days and nights blended into one endless darkened eternity, the light from the television dancing on the walls and my gooseflesh like fire ... religious channels with Southern preachers screaming about Lord Jesus and damnation ... shopping channels "...and now Jay, you say this superb pendant is only 99 dollars 99 cents?" ... canned laughter ... news "...the latest drug menace sweeping America..." I groaned and squirmed, the sheets wet with sweat and puke, and I begged for it to end ...

I awoke from the sickness the evening before I was due to fly from LAX, tired, sore and scared. Here I was again, kicked, lost and desperately trying to figure out where I went wrong last time. With my last night in Los Angeles looming ahead of me, I did, I suppose, all there was left to do. I carried on. I scored some crack and sat up all night in the motel room getting high, watching *In Living Color* reruns. In the morning I checked onto my flight weak, shaky and crashing hard from the coke.

The thirteen-hour flight was a living, gibbering Technicolor nightmare. Still sick and suicidal from kicking heroin, the come down from the crack started twisting objects in the edge of my field of vision into dark things, scary things. I sat rooted to my chair, wired yet aching for sleep, jumping and knocking my tray into the air when a stewardess walked past me unexpectedly, sweating profusely and stinking of cocaine and withdrawal sweat. The fat, pasty English guy in the seat next to me snarled in visible disgust at my appearance and I drummed my fingers, nervously caressing the needle sores on my forearm, praying for the flight to end.

As the plane drew closer to England I felt as if I was being led into a death chamber. I was returning with nothing, with years of my life completely lost in a blizzard of drugs. I tried to get drunk but felt only tired and sick from the whiskey.

The skies over Heathrow were grey, wet and ominous. And I wanted a shot of heroin more than I had ever wanted one in my life.

LONDON, AGAIN

So that was how I returned to London, like a beaten dog: broke, depressed and full of regrets. Goodbye Los Angeles and hello to London, again, in January 2001, one of the coldest winters on record. Sleeping on friends' floors and in abandoned buildings, the cold cutting through the few clothes I had taken with me, my money dwindling fast, taking interviews for a series of menial jobs with a CV full of lies for people who didn't care. Back to that same old UK drag, the worst kind of drag there is. A bring-down, the whole fucking country was a bring-down and soon I needed drugs to help with the boredom and the poverty and the cold and the having to wake up every fucking morning and hop across the ice cold bedsit I rented for 55 quid a week to let a trickle of warm water run over my body. Watching spiders and mice crawl around the place, on the bus in the rain Albercrombie Mansions, broken tiles and pools of water in the foyer. Fried chicken – more fried chicken than in the whole of the U.S. I imagine, Tennessee Fried Chicken, Delicious Fried Chicken, Orlando Fried Chicken, halal chicken, kosher chicken, unfit for human consumption chicken, sullen Arab boys flipping burgers and pouring mayonnaise on French fries and AA meetings in church halls and basements and community centres listening to the same old talk, the same old lies and the same old twelve-step misery. Kids too young to know any better attending because they think they smoke too much weed or drink too much, beaten down-looking Kings Cross prostitutes trying to stay off the needle for their screaming children's sake, smack and crack dealers trying to stop and not knowing how sitting around in a circle talking about deals they did and runs they have had, all of them with the look of someone who just awoke from a coma to a world they no longer belong in.

187

It ended for me in Camden, sitting around in one of those churches looking for a likely face and one guy in particular had the look of a reluctant junky about him—sallow cheeks, big scared eyes, pale skin, didn't want to say much. I could tell that it was over for him as well, that he was just waiting for a reason to jack in all of this self-help fellowship companionship, finding it as empty as I found it, so I decided to give him his reason. We talked, I told him what was up and in an hour we had made a connection and were up in his flat, cooking up the brown powder in lemon juice, tying off and shooting our way back to glory.

I shoplifted from markets mostly—Camden, Portobello, Spitalfields—to get the clothes I needed to stay warm. I lived in a series of short let apartments all over the city: Shepherds Bush, White City, Tufnell Park, Hackney, all cheap and cold and miserable. My health wasn't good, my teeth starting to fall out, one while eating a steak and another snapping off into the crust of a pizza. My parents coming through with a hundred here or there when it seemed like I was at rock bottom, my heroin habit growing again with alarming regularity. January moved into February and then March, the winter seemingly endless. I sat there on many long nights thinking of ending it all in a rat bag flat in the East End shooting heroin and cocaine and going crazy with melancholy. The idea of getting onto a methadone program started to loom on the horizon again, but after my experience in Hollywood, I was wary, to say the least.

Finally I found myself with no other option, no money and no prospect of money for a while. I walked into a GP's surgery, hearing that this particular doctor was willing to prescribe methadone and I laid it on the line. I was broke, sick, out of credit with my dealer and with no idea of how I was going to get through the day. I had started a new job selling ad space for a music magazine and I knew that if I didn't get a prescription today that I would lose the job and possibly my apartment. I begged and cajoled. The doctor was doubtful, but someone had just that morning dropped out of the methadone program and there was a place and somehow I got it. I started off on eighty ml of the sweet tasting green linctus a day and began trying to put

188

my life back into order.

It was hard, crawling back. I often thought that I might never make it. The hardest thing about being on a methadone program is not abstaining from heroin but restraining yourself from physically attacking the doctors, caseworkers and pharmacists who all conspire to make your life impossible. Doctors who tell you that you are mentally ill and in need of years of therapy to confront your inner demons. Caseworkers (basically glorified social workers with little or no medical knowledge) who tell you that they do not believe a word you say as all junkies are by their very nature liars and you are no exception. Pharmacists who dispense your methadone with a sneer and remind you not to steal anything while you are waiting to get dosed. All of them assholes, all of them shits with an axe to grind, all of them with the power to have your prescription taken away from you at twenty-four hours notice. It is not a very secure feeling, knowing that the whim of any of these people involved in your treatment could leave you out in the cold, with a bigger habit that you had coming into the program (methadone is notoriously harder to withdraw from than heroin). You start to find yourself sitting around in chemists' shops waiting to score instead of car parks and coffee shops, but it's always the same deal. The connection—be they the dealer or the pharmacy—will make you wait. You always have to wait. They will belittle you and you will always have to respond to them with a smile and the suitable amount of ingratiating grovelling. At least when you are using street drugs you can always find another connection straight away. With methadone, one stink at any drug dependency unit or GP's office will follow you around, thwarting your every attempt to even get on another waiting list like a curse from an evil eye. Suddenly, on methadone the walls begin to close in around you and you are left with two stark choices—submit to this life or get clean.

Submitting at first seems like the easy option. It's just a matter of keeping up the routine, keeping up the pretence. People are nice to people that they detest every day in every walk of life, so why is doing it to your doctor any different? Maybe in two years, if you behave yourself, they will let you attend the clinic less regularly. Maybe you will be able to pick up your methadone weekly instead of daily. Maybe they'll ask to watch you piss into a bottle less than they do now.

It's no way to live though, and you realize that. It's patently obvious when you speak to the guys who have been on a 'script for most of their lives. They are older now, fatter, too, with the pallor of the methadone addict and a sheen of sweat constantly on their brow. Some of them jump like a startled animal when their numbers are called to see their caseworker, someone who will be, in all probability, some asshole straight out of college who has never so much as smoked a joint. And you sit there, thinking of the stories they have told you—the years of scoring and hustling and avoiding jails and morgues—and you know that despite their lifetime of experience they will still have to postulate themselves in front of this young halfwit in order to keep up the charade of conviviality needed to retain their methadone. Even the ones who hold their nerve and don't jump still have that look in their eyes, the startled look of someone wondering how it came to this ... years of cramming down hurt and pain deep down inside yourself. They are men with the weight of the world—or at least the medical establishment—on their shoulders.

Withdrawal though, it's all about withdrawal. The withdrawal from methadone is just as severe as from heroin, with the added horror of it lasting for two weeks or more. Despite all of the reasons you have for not wanting to stay on methadone, that fear of withdrawal is one that brushes aside all other concerns. So you remain trapped in indecision, knowing that if you ask the clinic to start reducing your medication it will be incredibly difficult to get them to stop and impossible to get your dose put back up to its original level. Misjudge that and you will be sicker and more screwed than ever. Months pass and the chances are you will remain tortured and undecided until the day you realize you are now one of these old, beat men waiting for their new 'script. That is, of course, unless something extraordinary happens.

And it did. I fell in love.

Vanessa was beautiful, probably the most beautiful looking girl I had ever seen. She was from New York, with gorgeous South American features and smooth caramel skin. We talked and laughed and fucked together in an innocent and happy way and every time I saw her it blew my mind that this amazing girl wanted to spend time with me. Her appearance in my life was as sudden and as forceful as that first appearance of heroin had been years earlier. Her presence shocked my out my dumb, methadone passivity.

As our relationship developed, the schism between the normality of our relationship and my life as a methadone patient started to grow. First I stopped injecting heroin, black market methadone or coke on top of my allotted dose. Although she claimed not to be bothered by the sight of my digging for veins in my arms and legs first thing in the morning while trying to get well enough to make it to the methadone clinic, I knew it had to be profoundly disturbing for a non-injector to watch. I started going out again to clubs and bars, snorting coke, dropping ecstasy and getting drunk. It was a new world in London and it had been rumbling on underneath my nose the whole time; music was exciting again, creativity was in the air, the seeds of legends were being sown in East End bars and venues. And despite having almost completely stopped all other drugs since becoming a heroin addict, I found that I still got a kick out of them. As I started meeting and gaining mutual friends with Vanessa, I realized that there had to me more for me than life as a methadone patient.

Regaining a sense that maybe life had something to offer me, I decided to come off of methadone and try again. Within a year of meeting Vanessa, I had switched to a drug called buprenorphine in order to withdraw altogether. I got a private doctor who prescribed me enough pills to kick at home and we did it together in our flat in Stoke Newington, me groaning and cursing myself for having to do this again and her doling out the pills, words of encouragement, kisses on my forehead ...

It was a month before I could do anything but chew Valium, smoke weed and watch television. The depression threatened to swallow me whole; I cried over charity appeals on television, I dreamt of shooting up and smoking crack as vividly as I had during my first month in rehab three years ago. I thought that my brain would never let me feel normal again.

In the midst of this depression I received a phone call from a ghost. Kat was on the other end of a crackly transatlantic connection, the first time I had spoken to her in years. She had tracked down my number after hearing I was in London and it was almost physically shocking to hear her voice again.

"I've got some bad news," she told me.

I hung up the phone half an hour later, exhausted and upset. RP had died in a motorcycle accident in Cambodia. After I had lost contact with him he started smoking crack heavily and it soon became the focus of his life. He started showing up on film sets for work cracked out and insane and people simply stopped hiring him. Kat recalled literally packing his bags and putting him on a plane to Cambodia to visit Sal Mackenzie and clean up. Out there his health improved, he met a girl and was even talking of starting a business and staying permanently. Then one night, driving at full throttle, with his girl riding on the back of the bike and Sal following, he rounded a corner and came upon an abandoned truck and in a flash of endless white light, it was over.

I thought of us in the same city, me in a motel bathroom and RP in his apartment in Echo Park locked into our private miseries, not knowing we would never speak again. Life felt fragile and transitional.

The word processor had been hiding away in the bottom of the wardrobe since Vanessa and I had moved in together. Even looking at it sometimes, I got an odd queasy feeling in my guts— it was stained with years old blood splatters and the writing inside was stained with something darker and far more permanent. I eventually dug it out the day that Vanessa told me she was pregnant.

In a way I was amazed that the rickety machine still worked. Flicking through the files contained in there I saw title upon title of failed video treatments for failed bands. I clicked on one and read the opening line: *"We are at a pool party on top of a mansion in the Hollywood Hills... the camera pulls back from a close-up shot of a bottle of Cristal..."* and I immediately clicked it off in disgust. I felt a dry heave building in my stomach and had the sense that this was a bad idea and I should leave well enough alone. Put the fucking thing back in the bottom of the wardrobe and take more Valium. Sleep. Watch some TV. Anything but this shit. I forced my attention back to the glow of the black and white screen.

I avoided any files that looked remotely related to my old line of work. I found clumsy attempts at poetry next. Awful—kid stuff. The ravings of a half-wit junky moron. A suicide note that I never finished which ended cryptically *"I'm fucked, tired, used up. I tried, but I can't do it anymore. I can't stay straight and I can't live like this. At least looking back I can say that I"* I guess I ran aground trying to come up with any achievements worth boasting about, or I nodded out at that point. More junk, bullshit, ravings. Then a short, four page description of the night that Suzie OD'd on coke. It was pretty good. When I finished it the dry heaves started again and I had to sit in the bathroom splashing water on my face for a while. I hadn't thought of that night in a while and had no recollection of writing about it, but out of anything I had written it was the best; it was to the point, and intentionally or not I had conjured that night with a perfect dead - eyed junky clarity.

I looked at the back of my hands; they were all I had now. I had been working since returning to London for the only people who would hire me: alcoholic lunatics running folk music magazines out of their basements, drug addicts running start up businesses into the ground, sales jobs for minimum wage, working underneath bitter, sadistic, asshole managers. I had an educational history that ended abruptly at eighteen years old and a work history as patchy as they come. These hands had once promised so much, now they were covered in still healing track marks, and the shiny scars denoting long-since calcified veins. Not hands to be proud of. Hands that had grown soft and weak through misuse. Could they ever do anything for me again?

I got up and walked to the window. I looked at the London skies, overcast and moody, the same skies that my as yet unborn child would soon look upon. I remembered my father's hands, how solid they seemed when I was a child, how sturdy. Hands that had laid concrete, driven busses, fixed cars. I looked at my hands again, white and thin and mangled. What good had these hands ever done?

With a sigh I walked over to the word processor, opened a blank document and began to write.

The first good night happened some time after, when Vanessa and I were at a party in Brixton where I met Jonathan, a friend of Vanessa's who had also left Los Angeles and junk behind. We talked and drank for at least four hours, talking about our relative experiences, the drug scene in Los Angeles and the difficulties he had coming off, too. He was no more interested in abstaining from all drugs than I was, yet here he was—fiercely intelligent, beautifully dressed, and most definitely no longer a junky, champagne glass in his hand, fixing me in a green eyed stare and telling me, "It does get better, you have to remember that it does get better." And I started to believe him. I realized that for the first time the alcohol was acting on my body in the desired way and I was happy instead of tired, loud and laughing instead of withdrawn and feeling ill. Almost as if on cue with meeting this other ex junky, my metabolism had somehow shifted, allowing me a glimpse of what wonders my body could experience if allowed to recover fully.

That night we all stumbled from the club drunk and happy into a warm Brixton night, a full champagne flute still in my hand, our drunken raucous laughter echoing up Coldharbor Lane, and I wrapped my arms around Vanessa and kissed her on the lips, tenderly, shocking her with a kind of intimacy that I had been unable to muster ever since coming off of opiates.

"I love you," I told her. "It's all going to be alright."

And on we went, until later we lay wrapped up together sleeping gently. It's all going to be alright.

194

LONDON, 2003

NO more junky talk, no more dope talk, no more quantifying my existence... How much smack? How much $$$? No more standing around in parking lots, in doctor's waiting rooms, on street corners waiting for the connection ... London, Los Angeles, San Francisco, here he is with his junky walk. Here comes Paco, here comes Henry, here comes Pedro, here comes Raphael, here comes TJ, here comes Richie ... down all the years, all the hours, all the streets and all of the places I have stood in solitary agony waiting for someone to drop a few hours peace into my hands.

Happy birthday to me. Twenty-three today. Standing in Kings Cross trying to score before I have to meet my friends for a birthday drink that I don't want. Before I have to be nice to people who don't know that I can't feel what they feel. Extra methadone warms my bones ... take me back to dear old Blighty.

Finally scored for a rock from some Rastafarian scam artist, tell him that if it's good I want more. Immediately tries to get me to buy more now. Refuse. Takes me to his car for a smoke. Asks me to give him the rock he sold me, and tosses it out of the window.

"That one," he says, "is bullshit."

There is no acknowledgement of the easy admission he has made. Pulls a real rock out of his mouth, and we drive around the corner and pick up his girlfriend who is streetwalking outside of a transient rooming house behind an amusement arcade. It is four o'clock in the afternoon. She jumps in, produces a crack pipe fashioned out of a miniature Martell cognac bottle from a fake Louis Vuitton purse.

We park up and we smoke the rock in the car. A police car rounds behind us checking out street traffic, waves of black dark paranoia fill the car as the guy pulls out and we drive around the

195

block partially tailed by the police. Somehow they lose interest. I am high, anxious and I haven't eaten all day. We agree on the deal, he sells me the other rock and I get out. I go into the McDonalds and lock myself in the bathroom to check my purchase. I have been burnt, sold nothing but layer upon layer of cellophane. I walk out. Through the glass front of the McDonalds I see Michael, a guy who used to attend the same Narcotics Anonymous meeting as me in Camden. I haven't seen him since I stopped attending. He is waiting by a newsstand, the furtive look of a man waiting for the connection. All around are people, all waiting, all pained and shifting from foot to foot in a conga line of misery ... happy birthday to me.

No more junk talk, no more lies. No more mornings in the hospital getting bad blood drained out of me. No more doctors trying to analyse what makes me a drug addict. No more futile attempts at trying to control my heroin use. No more defending myself when I know I am practically indefensible. No more police, using me as practice. No more ODs, no more losses. No more trying to take an intellectual position on my heroin addiction when it takes more than it gives. No more dope-sick mornings, no more slow suicide, no more pain without end.

No more AA. No more NA. No more CA. No more mind control. No more being a victim, no more looking for reasons in childhood, in God in anything but what exists in HERE. No more admitting I am powerless.

Down the dusty Los Angeles sidewalks, down the urine stained London back alleys ... there goes the connection fading into the crowd like a 1960's Polaroid.

"Business...?"

"Whachoo need...?"

"Chiva...?"

Tony O'Neill

London, October 21st 2003

196